MENACE

The Death Dealer

Written by Steve Samedi

Glover Lane Press
Publishers Since January 2000
www.gloverlanepress.webs.com

MENACE; The Death Dealer

Copyright © 2014-2015 by Steve Samedi

ISBN-13: 978-0692352182
ISBN-10: 069235218X

Edited by Tammy Young

Cover Design by Azaan Kamau

The Mission of Glover Lane Press is to Uplift, Empower, Elevate the Masses and Provide American Jobs. Every book published by Glover Lane Press and it's many imprints, is printed and manufactured in the United States of America, ensuring and maintaining American employment.

DEDICATION

Menace: The Death Dealer is dedicated to the loving memory of my grandmother, Andrea Marie Samedi. She was the person who knew me the best. I wish she could have lived to see this day but I know God had other plans. Her legacy will continue to live on through her children, grandchildren and great-grandchildren.

SPECIAL THANKS

I would like to thank everyone who encouraged me throughout this process. I didn't know what I was doing at first and had some really rough, rough drafts. The support of my friends and family was a motivating force that I relied upon. When I began this process I could not have imagined the late night tying sessions, heavy research and countless revisions. I doubted in my abilities as a writer and considered quitting many times. This book is a testament to the faith my loved ones had in me. Thank you.

Special thanks to my Mom and Dad, for raising me to be an independent and creative thinker, my brother and sister, Graig and Nadege, for listening to my ideas and nixing the bad ones. Amber Washington who introduced me to Glover Lane Publishing and my unofficial editors: Samantha Brown, Verdell Wright and Patrick Rogers, I truly appreciate your assistance.

Special thanks to all my supporters including but not limited to: Danielle Gille, Rocener Gille, Roceny Gille, Tempestt Dickerson, Ben Napoleon, Dyson Evans, Duchana Gille, Marjory Vilme Wilkinson, Erinn Wilkinson, Gregory Vilme, Beatrice Vilme, Maudeline Jean, Marie Alexis, Henderson Alexis, Fabienne Euphrasie, Tyron Hayes, Alfonso Alicea, Tiffany Jackson, Alton Moore, Rene Gordon, Marion Ricks, Tyree Cooper, Diandra Kaufman, Jamaal Armstrong, Jennifer Porto, Paola Ricardo, Neesha Gunnis, Devin Brown, Chris Brown, Joanne Pennington, Tanika Martin, Tanesia Tanner, Chelsea Horvath, Trisha

Farrier, Angela Nicolosi, Kris Hlatky, Raafe Islam, Keegan Rollins, Brian Rottkamp, Michael McClain, Olivia Zangani, Kevin Woolfolk and last but not least Azaan Kamau and all the GLP staff.

CONTENTS

CHAPTER 1

DEAD END, NEW BEGINNING

Death was once a stranger to me, but now we're intimately acquainted. She was just an abstract concept until I lost someone close. Then, Death became as real as a table, a chair—even a kiss. Before my mother's death, I thought I knew who I was and where I was going. Then, a year ago, I learned that I knew nothing about my life, my family or my destiny.

The day that changed everything began like so many others. I stopped by the store on my way home from work, picked up some milk for my Lucky Charms, and made my way passed the graffiti littered storefront. I wiped my feet on the welcome mat, checked both pockets for my keys and opened the front door. As usual, I checked the answering machine. A red number one was flashing. *Beep.* The voice coming from the machine was completely unfamiliar.

A man with a thick Japanese accent introduced himself, "Hello, I am Kenzan Kaito." Hesitating, he continued, "I am a friend of your father's." I could tell by the tone of his voice that something was wrong. "I have something important to share with you. Please contact me as soon as you get this message." He left me a number where I could reach him. I stood there, unable to dial wondering what type horrors laid in Pandora's Box. My fingers reluctantly pressed each digit as if I was disarming a bomb. The seconds before I heard a voice felt like an eternity.

"Hello."

"This is Phillip Baxter," I replied.

"Thank you for returning my call, Phillip. There's no right way to give you this news. I am sorry to tell you this, but your father is dead."

My heart dropped. Kenzan informed me that my dad had been killed in an apparent carjacking. It was an inexplicable feeling of sadness, anger, and shock. My father had lived in Japan for years. He conducted business there. He had even grown up there, but I had little to no connection with the man or that country. Kenzan assured me that everything would be taken care of for me. As the conversation ended, he once again expressed his extreme sadness in having to deliver such terrible news.

Kenzan made the arrangements for my father's funeral. It was to be held in a village just outside of Tokyo. I had lived in Philadelphia all of my life and had not traveled much at that point, yet I flew across the world to bury a man I had barely known. It had been over a year since my mother's funeral. She had been in a terrible car accident on her way home from work—her life cut short by a drunk driver. Out of respect, my father flew back from Tokyo to attend her funeral. I thought it would be our chance to finally develop a lasting bond. He knew I needed him more than ever, yet he acted as if he was oblivious to what I was going through. He stayed around for a few days before returning to Japan. I never would have guessed that it would be the last time I saw him.

The next few days were almost unbearable for me. Everyone asked me why I continued to go to work. The truth was I didn't want to be alone with my thoughts. By this point, I was used to having my decisions questioned, second-guessed even stymied. My father was a fairly wealthy man. He owned a successful movie production company. However, he wasn't the parent whose path I decided to follow in. I wanted to be a teacher, like my mother. I had been able to witness her impact on young people's lives. I loved history and was working on my Masters in Education, while working as a substitute teacher at local high schools to make money. My friends had expected me to sit back and receive a cushy job from my "Pops," but I had not been raised to rely on anyone for assistance—especially my father. I could not blame my coworkers for their assumptions, however; there was no way for them to comprehend the complexity of our relationship.

The buzzing of the alarm clock startled me the morning of my dreaded flight. I rechecked my luggage to make sure I hadn't forgotten anything. My cab arrived, I stuffed my bags into the trunk, and we made our way to the airport. I could tell that the driver wanted to spark up a conversation by his random comment on the nice weather. It was July after all, and for once we weren't in the midst of a heat wave. He must've taken notice of my solemn demeanor, as he responded with deafening silence.

Arriving at Philadelphia International I thanked the driver with a wad of crumpled bills. I had been in such a rush to make it to the airport on time I'd forgotten to get anything to eat. I knew I had a long flight ahead of me, so I got a coffee and a cream-cheese bagel. Seconds later, the announcement of my flight was made and I boarded the plane. I was disappointed in my aisle seat; I figured I'd end up being bumped by everyone who passed by me. I squeaked out just enough space to fit my bag into the overhead compartment.

I was seated next to an older gentleman and woman, presumably his wife. We made some small talk about our impending trips. The couple had been retired for several years, and now spent a considerable amount of their time traveling the world. When the conversation got around to my reasons for traveling to Japan, the mood quickly deflated. I explained how I was only visiting there to bury my dad. They showed concern for my loss, which I obviously appreciated.

The fifteen-hour flight awarded me abundant time to reflect. I was in a situation where I could not escape my thoughts. My emotions were conflicted; I was a slightly more mad than sad. It felt terrible to think that way about a dead man.

Did I mention that my dad and I shared the same name? I'm actually the third in the line of Phillip Theodore Baxter. Sharing that name with my father was pouring salt into an open wound. Why would you give your son your name, and then abandon him? It was a constant reminder that I was my father's son. That statement may sound stupid, but it was how I felt. So much of your identity is tied into the name you've been given. I guess I had never dealt with my deep-rooted feelings of insecurity.

I think the problem was that no one had talked about him at all. My mom thought she was sparing me from the awkward conversations. Throughout my childhood, she'd done her best not to diminish my father in my eyes. She had made excuse after excuse for his absence, when she really didn't have to. She'd wanted me to form my own opinion of him as a man. As a result, she had also given me no impression of the man she'd fallen in love with.

The one thing I can say for my dad is that he had tried to support us financially, though his financial contribution had not been enough to substitute for his willful negligence. My mother had been abandoned, forced to raise a man on her own. She could expect a check here and there to pay for stuff like clothes and food. As a kid, I'd thought I was the only one in pain but over time I'd learned how his absence affected both of us negatively.

My mother never seriously recovered from having her heart broken. What was worse was, I resembled my dad more and more as I got older. On some level I knew that my presence alone was a reminder of what she had lost. My mom had never even changed her last name. She'd never put effort into dating, either, or on building any type of romantic relationship. She worked long hours, sometimes a second job, to provide for us. She only accepted money from my dad because she thought it would be unfair to punish me for his actions.

In my neighborhood, it had been rare for a child to have a father around. I soon learned that my dad's absence wasn't unique to my family's situation. As a young black kid in Philly I was considered lucky that he gave us any support. I didn't feel lucky; I thought I deserved a real father and a real relationship. Deep down, I believed we would have our chance to build a relationship. I was scared to be the one to make the first step, though; I needed him to make the effort. The last thing I wanted to do was to open myself up for more rejection. Now I was faced with the realization that the chance had been taken out of both our hands.

As scheduled, the plane touched down at Haneda Airport in less than fifteen hours. I collected my luggage and went through customs. As I exited the airport, I saw a chauffeur holding up a sign with my name. I looked around to see if anyone else had seen this man. I had never been in a limo before in my life. I slowly approach the driver, who looked to be very nervous.

From our brief encounter, my driver, William, seemed like a really nice man. He spoke English fluently with a slight accent, which was a relief since I did not speak Japanese. He opened the door for me while motioning for me to take a seat. Once inside the limo, I felt the cold leather as it brushed up against my skin. For a moment I wanted to pinch myself, to establish a sense of reality. William brought it to my attention that I'd be staying in one of the nicest hotels in Tokyo.

As we moved through the city I was amazed by how familiar it all seemed. This sprawling metropolis could have been Times Square, yet it contained a flair that was uniquely Japanese. I was engrossed by the activities in the large shopping district, from the gigantic screens and neon lights to the eccentric assortment of people. It was a shame that I was only here under such negative circumstances.

We parked in front of the Idemas Hotel, located in the heart of Shinjuku, Tokyo. It was more beautiful than I could have imagined. As I stepped out of the limo I was blinded by the sun's glare reflecting off the multitude of windows. The hotel had to be fifty stories high, with hundreds of rooms. At this time I was beginning to notice how much I stood out in this country. It had now been almost a day since I'd seen anyone who remotely resembled me. It's funny how much you notice, when you're taken out of your home environment.

The clerk at the desk recognized my name, and expressed sadness over my loss. I hadn't been unaware of my father's high status in Japan. A few whispers ballooned into a small scene, as guests began to make the connection. I quickly got out of the lobby and into the elevator. I felt a sense of relief to finally be in my room. I was told that my room had been bumped up to the executive suite, which had a breathtaking view overlooking the skyscrapers of the Tokyo skyline. Leaning against the railing of the terrace, I tried to limit the painful thoughts of what should've been. You never come out a winner when you play a game of what-ifs.

CHAPTER 2

REVELATIONS

Not long after getting settled, I received a call from Kenzan. He had planned for the wake to be held at my father's home on the following day. I thought it would have been held at a funeral home, but I have to admit that I was curious to see where my father had lived. The time leading up to the wake seemed to fly by rapidly. The driver brought me to my father's home, located right outside the city in a neighborhood called, Yotsuya.

The other homes in Yotsuya were positioned very close together, juxtaposed to the Baxter residence, sitting on a secluded estate. The home was a white, square structure that almost looked transparent from the outside. The grounds had an intricate garden accentuated by two symmetrical cherry-blossom trees. Briefly, I allowed myself to be sidetracked by the allure and serenity of nature. I had been accustomed to the noisy, hectic bustle of the city life, and this was such a departure. I shifted my attention to the line of people I saw entering the home. The large windows enabled me to so see all the preparations from the outside. I could never have lived in a home that was so exposed. Either he had nothing to hide, or he had gone out of his way to appear as though he didn't.

I stepped through the front door and everything stopped, as if we were in a M. C. Escher painting. I don't know if I was more taken aback by the geometric configuration of the house or the reaction of the guests. My goal was to pay my respects, without having the entire room gawking and whispering right in front of my face. A man, wearing dark shades concealing a scar near his left eye, walked over from the casket and greeted me.

He offered his condolences first and introduced himself as Kenzan Kaito. "Phillip, it's an honor to finally meet you," he said. Kenzan bowed to me, and I stood in silence, unsure of how to react. Should I bow to him? Would he be offended if I bowed incorrectly? He smiled, assuring me that it was okay not to understand the customs. Mourners continued to file in, placing gift envelopes on the table stationed near the entrance. Kenzan explained that the attendants gave money to the family, as a way of paying respect to the dead.

The priest arrived, and many of the guests welcomed him. To my surprise, the priest took the time to come speak to me. Kenzan took it upon himself to assist with the translation. His uplifting and gracious words helped to ease the pain. By that time, everyone had been seated for the ceremony. There was a whole family section assigned for these ceremonies, but there was no family— just me, a glorified stranger carrying on his legacy. (I can't say that wasn't symbolic of how he had lived his life.)

The ceremony opened with a reading from the Buddhist scripture known as the *Amitabha Sutra*. Kenzan did his best to translate the readings and explain the proceedings to me. I participated in a ritual, which consisted of lighting incense and bowing before the body. As family I had the honor of being first to participate. Kenzan walked me through the process, and the others followed after me.

The service ended, but people continued to pay their respects. I asked Kenzan if this was normal, to which he replied, "No. Your father had a special relationship with these people." He explained that my father was held in such high regard for his impact on the community.

This was one of the rare times when someone had talked favorably about my father with me. I gained access to another man's perspective on his life. As a kid, I had imagined that my dad was off somewhere doing great things. I wanted so badly to have logical reasons to explain he had left our family. I was now comforted by the fact that he had managed to do some great things in his life after all.

This experience also stirred up a lot of old feelings I had thought were buried. I excused myself to go to the restroom. As I left, a woman advised me not to go into the room with the old-fashioned sliding doors. Things apparently weren't as transparent as the impression given from the outside.

In the bathroom, I finally let my guard down. The tears started rolling down my cheeks. I wiped my face feverishly, even though no one else could see me cry. I was shaken by a knock on the door. It was Kenzan, checking up on me. The man had somehow come upstairs without making a sound. He mentioned how some of the guests noticed my absence from the ceremony.

When we returned, he informed me of another Buddhist custom. In the Buddhist culture the family stays up with the body the night before the funeral. I thought it was a strange tradition and wasn't pleased. I knew the dead were revered in this culture; however I'd underestimated to what extent. This was akin to a cruel joke being played on me. I had no way of avoiding the body now.

I walked over to my father as he lay there in the casket. During the service I had done everything in my power to avoid looking straight at him. I studied his lifeless body, knowing we could never reconcile. Since the moment I had gotten there, people had been speaking highly of this man. What was it about Japan that had drawn my father there? Why was he such a great man to everyone, except to those who should have mattered most in the grand scheme of his life?

One must ask oneself if it is more important to have the respect of many or the love of the few. You can't change the ones you love, no matter how great your intention may be. I decided at that moment to forgive my father for his actions. This would be my last opportunity to make peace and put everything behind me. Buddhists believe that death is not the end of a life; it is the transition into a new state of being. Maybe this was my opportunity for a new beginning, too.

Kenzan and I traded stories about my father over the course of the evening. Sadly, he had many more stories to tell. I asked him what he thought about my father's noninvolvement in my life. This wasn't an attempt to change his opinion of my father; I just wanted his real opinion as his close friend.

"There was more to your father then you could ever know," he replied. "This is not the time for such things. I promise you that I will explain more after the funeral." His comments confused me, but I agreed to pursue it at a more appropriate time.

Kenzan suggested that I stay in Tokyo for a while. He felt that the only way to gain closure was to draw closer to my family legacy rather than breaking away from it. Our conversation stretched for so long we did not realize we'd been talking all night.

The morning of the funeral, the body was transported from the house to the temple where the funeral was to be held. The temple was similar to temples I had seen on television: Large staircase led up to the entrance, the roof had a pointed top, which slanted and flared outward, and red columns supported the structure, which had an upper and lower level.

I slid open the door and prepared myself for the ceremony. I fought to keep my composure. This time, many of the guests had rosaries, which they held in their hands. Once again, I was the first to walk over to the altar. I placed incense in the urn and then bowed to the other guests. As my father's only son, it was customary for me to thank everyone. It was weird trying to find the right words, considering that these people knew him much better than I did. Several attendants took time afterward, to offer words of encouragement and read some letters written to my father.

Out of the corner of my eye, I could swear that I saw someone very familiar. A young lady with a caramel complexion was facing the altar. She had shoulder-length hair and mesmerizingly large almond-colored eyes. She resembled my ex-girlfriend, Denise Leonard. That made about as much sense as anything else that was going on I figured. There were only a few Americans attending, so she stood out like a sore thumb. I had to get a closer look, but I was interrupted by the transportation of the body. The pallbearers lifted the casket, obstructing my view.

After they passed, I could no longer see the woman. They loaded the hearse with the casket as the concession took off to the crematorium. After a couple of hours waiting at the funeral home, I was given an urn containing my father's remains. His wish had been to have his ashes spread over the sea. Despite my reservations I felt obligated to honor that.

Did I want to return home to America, or should I stay a while longer? Some part of me wouldn't allow myself to just leave like that. I called the airlines and changed my flight plans. The one person who had the information I needed was here in Japan. With so much going on, it had slipped my mind that I had to attend my father's will reading. As I picked up the phone, coincidentally Kenzan was calling. He was relieved to have caught me when he did. He didn't want me to be late. People frown upon that, even more over there.

I had honestly wanted to avoid the lawyers and paperwork. I hadn't needed anything from him while he was alive, and I needed even less now. I had no stake in his company or in any of his other business ventures. Nevertheless, I was there on time because I didn't want to disappoint Kenzan. He and I had established a good rapport in the short time we had spent together. He enticed me to attend, but I countered with one stipulation: I wanted him to explain his cryptic message from the wake. If there was "more" to my father, I needed to know what that was.

By then I had become tired of all the limo riding. It had been exciting at first, but this wasn't me. I rationalized that it was a safer option than driving myself, since I had no experience driving on the left side of the road. As soon as I arrived at the office building, I was greeted by a group of lawyers. I extended my hand to shake theirs, and we made our way up the elevator.

We immediately got to business. My dad had left some money for charity, to his staff and of course to Mr. Kaito, who was awarded some stock and made the Chief Creative Officer at the studio. The lawyer addressed me last, stating this was the final section of the will. I had been awarded the majority of stock in Baxter Productions. He went on to name homes, cars, and other valuables my father had left for me.

I should have been excited, but I wasn't. I had no business being the owner of a company. I caught up with Kenzan as we exited the meeting and told him he had some explaining to do.

He quickly put his index finger up to his lips, and whispered, "Quiet! Not here. Come to my house tomorrow and I'll explain everything you want to know. Be at my home in exactly twenty-four hours."

Finally, I was about to get some answers.

I arrived exactly twenty-four hours later. I walked right up to the door of the address he gave me. Kenzan had a relatively small home compared to my father's. I knocked on the door two or three times. He greeted me and invited me in.

Kenzan asked me to remove my shoes at the door. The shoes were placed on a rack near the front door. "You have a very lovely home," I said.

He thanked me and offered me a seat. I asked if he lived there alone. He told me he used to be married, but that his wife had left him long ago. His children had also moved to the states many years back. He spent most of his time working with my father and also ran a martial arts studio where he taught. I felt like I was getting a glimpse at another side of Kenzan, which was actually pretty cool.

Kenzan talked about some hit movies he had worked on. I'd had no idea my father had been involved in some of my favorite action films. He offered me some tea, to which I agreed. As he was leaving the room, he handed me a photo album, which was filled with childhood pictures of him and my dad. I had had no idea they'd been close for that long.

He returned to find me standing in front of his mantle looking at his awards. "Let's get to the issues at hand," he said. I nodded in agreement and returned to my seat.

He cleared his throat as if to stall for every last possible second. Kenzan had sworn to break his silence only upon my father's death. My father had done some terrible things of which he was not proud. He'd done things that would get a man put in prison for his entire life. I assumed he was referring to some shady business practices. If only it had been so simple.

"What kind of things?" I asked.

Kenzan looked at me for a moment, took a deep breath, and then cut right to the chase. "Well, your father used to kill people, and do it very well. Yeah, he was basically the Da Vinci of killing people. He was a mercenary of the highest caliber, a death dealer."

I was understandably confused about what I was hearing. He noticed the stunned look on my face. He tried to reassure me that everything was not so black and white, but I wasn't buying it. A killer was a killer; I didn't care for a distinction. However, I was holding out for anything that could explain my father's actions. I wanted so badly to give him the benefit of the doubt. This added information, though, did nothing to paint a better picture.

Not only was he a bad father, but he was also a wanted man. I did not see how this revelation was meant to endear me to my father. I couldn't help but laugh at what I heard, and the laugh was almost reflexive.

I asked if there was more, or was the whole "mercenary thing" the last of it?

According to Kenzan, there was more, and somehow I knew I was not going to like it. "Your father was far more involved in your life than you were aware of," he said. He went on to reveal that my father had people around me, watching me and guarding me. His lifestyle had been dangerous, and he worked for ruthless businessmen. Any one of them could have targeted his son, and he had to protect his legacy. I was not given the opportunity to ponder the implications.

"Do you know a woman named, Denise Leonard?" Kenzan asked. I acknowledged our former association, but my thought process remained obtuse. Denise and I had dated for about a year before my mother died. Things had gotten rocky after her death and I am man enough to admit that I pushed her away. It was one of the biggest mistakes of my life. Since that time I hadn't built or maintained any close relationships.

"She was raised in this home from a very young age. Denise is like a daughter to me," Kenzan further explained. His implications became more than clear. My father had hired her, as my personal bodyguard was the only logical conclusion I could reach. Suddenly, I saw the relationship in another light. My father had sent a beautiful woman my way, and I had fallen for his trap. I must have been so easy for her to manipulate. She just batted her eyelashes and giggled at my jokes. Even after we had broken up, she had remained one of my closest friends and confidants. I thought our bond had transcended our romantic past, but now I see it had all been an act.

The truth was, she had been one of Mr. Kaito's best students. They had trained together for many years in his dojo. My father had needed someone close, someone who could get closer than any man would. What scared me now was that he had to know the type of girl I preferred to pull off this level of deception. Denise had the looks, personality and attitude that I found irresistible. Still, how could he have known that it would work? This might not have been the only time he had tried this. Could I trust anyone who had been in my life, besides my mother?

I now made the connection as to why she had attended my father's funeral. Denise must have really cared for him to risk being seen there by me. "Where is Denise?" I asked him. He didn't answer. "She had made me feel like a jerk for breaking up with her, when she'd been playing me from the get-go," I said.

These revelations hit me hard. At that point, I needed to get away from everyone so I excused myself abruptly. I hopped in the limo and asked the driver to take me back to the hotel.

On the drive into the city I saw all kinds of people in the shopping district. I was overtaken by the compulsion to get out. I wasn't a limo-riding rich kid; I was the kid who walked home from school and took the bus until I was twenty. I asked the driver to stop. He must have not taken me seriously because he kept on driving.

"Stop the limo!" I yelled, "Let me out!" We came to a screeching halt, and I was bucked forward towards the back of the passenger's seat. The door unlocked; I opened it, got out and began to walk with no intended destination.

Not a minute went by before people started to notice me. I did my best to work my way through the small crowd of onlookers. I kept walking for close to an hour, before something stopped me in front of a fashion boutique. The frenzied customers confronted me with questions, and some even wanted to take pictures. Some of them knew who I was; others probably thought I was an American musician.

Out of my peripheral view, I saw a gorgeous Japanese woman shopping at the far end of the boutique. She paid me no mind as she picked out another pair of designer jeans. I was intrigued by this woman though, and felt I had to make her acquaintance. The hordes of people were clumped in front of the entranceway. I worked the crowd until I got to the door. I looked both ways, but it was as if she had vanished. There was no way she could've gotten through the crowd. It seemed like nothing was going right for me. I had some money on me, so I took a cab back to my hotel.

CHAPTER 3

SINS OF THE PAST

Lamentations 5:7

Our ancestors sinned, but they have died—
and we are suffering the punishment they deserved!
New Living Translation

An unexpected guest stopped by my hotel room two days after my discussion with Kenzan. A CIA agent by the name of Adrian Cole flashed a shiny badge at the door. I invited the man in and seated him in the living room area. Agent Cole interrogated me about the mysterious circumstances surrounding my father's death and showed me a series of pictures. In his opinion, it appeared to have been a premeditated murder and not a random street crime. Agent Cole kept saying, "Something doesn't seem right here," as he ran his fingers through his slick, pompadour hair.

The carjacking story did not lineup with the evidence found at the scene of the crime. I denied ever laying eyes on the men he presented and Agent Cole's frustration became clear. The disappointed agent had no choice but to move on with his investigation. He left a number where I might reach him and told me to call it if I ran into any trouble.

Immediately, I called Kenzan and told him about my run-in with the CIA agent. Kenzan alleged that in 20 years, neither he nor my father had any run-ins with law enforcement of any kind. We had to assume that the CIA's investigation had passed the infancy stage and our phones might've been tapped. With that in mind, we planned to reconvene the following day at his dojo.

I was afraid of what the CIA might find. A mercenary is not a typical nine-to-five profession. Dad could have been an international criminal for all I knew. The man juggled a double life and I wanted to know if he had brought danger to my front door.

Kenzan was scheduled to instruct a children's martial arts class until 3:00 pm. In an effort not to inconvenience him, I made arrangements to meet up after the class. It was also a great way to see him in a different context, specifically in his own element. I purposely arrived early so that I could catch a glimpse at the end of the class.

Seeing the children in his class, took me back to my childhood. I took a few years of karate after my father suggested it in one of our brief phone conversations. I used to be one of the smallest boys in my class growing up. A bully continually harassed me on my walk home from school. I tried to keep it from my mother but she figured it out somehow. I guess some would call it "motherly intuition." My mother enrolled me in a karate class to learn self-defense and to build my confidence. It had been uncharacteristic of my father to push for anything so hard. Now, it makes sense considering what I had uncovered.

I observed the lesson from the entrance hall, trying not to disturb the class. To my surprise, Denise was teaching the class not Kenzan. I watched her instruct the children on proper form and technique. By chance, she looked up and saw me standing in the back of the room. She was visibly shaken by my mere presence. Denise attempted to regain her composure and continued to teach the class after a moment of confusion. At the end, she thanked everyone for a good class as she walked the parents and students to the exit. For less than a minute, only the two of us remained in the room. We stood there, face-to-face, yet nothing was uttered. Denise opened her mouth, but the only thing to leave her lips was a breath. I was the first one to speak, even surprising myself.

"Hi, Denise. Didn't expect to run into you at the dojo. I have an appointment with your boss."

Our relationship was revealed to be part of her cover so I treated her like a spy, not as a friend or former girlfriend.

"Phillip, I--," were the only words she mustered before being interrupted.

Kenzan burst out of his office and Denise took the opening to retreat from the tense situation. He walked over to a closet, pulled out two brown leather books and handed them to me.

"What's this?" I asked.

"These journals belonged to your father and grandfather. They contain the personal accounts of their exploits. No doubt, they'll provide any information you'll need. Go home and read these as if your life depended on it. Come back with any questions you might have."

"It's going to take a while to read through these thick books. Can you at least give me a preview so I can understand what I've gotten myself into?"

"I still struggle to speak of the terrible things we were a part of. It would be best if you read it yourself and come up with your own conclusions."

Kenzan asked how much I knew about my grandfather. There wasn't much to be said except that he was a Vietnam vet who died a couple of years before I was born.

"Your family history has a lot of twists and turns." He said. "I believe I've pieced together the whole story. Your father inherited the mercenary identity from him about 25 years ago. My advice is to read your grandfather's journal first. Trust me."

He wished me luck and sent me on my way. I got back to the hotel and flipped open to the first page of the worn-out journal. My hands trembled as I began reading my grandfather's innermost thoughts.

Grandpa, the first Phillip Baxter, was a warrant officer who served in Vietnam for 7 years. The Vietnam War had been a devastating experience for many veterans, my grandpa included. In the 1960s, the country was in the midst of the civil rights movement and everyone had a cause worth fighting for or against. America got involved in a war on the other side of the world to stop the spread of Communism. Grandpa had just gotten married when he was drafted in 1966. He hated to leave his wife but he looked forward to what he could accomplish in the army. He relished the opportunity to fight for America and to prove that colored folks had an equal stake in their country's future.

No one foresaw the impact the war would have on the lives of these men. The fighting was brutal, unlike anything we've witnessed as a nation. Everything was undefined from the battlefield to the opposing forces. America was on their turf and the Vietcong used home field advantage quite effectively.

Over the years, the troops gained familiarity with the cultural quirks of the local people. A standout feature of the culture had been their love of card games. Rumblings swirled in the camps concerning the Vietcong's supposed death card superstitions. (The ace of spade was the "death card" and many believed that its presence on a dead body would haunt the spirit in the afterlife.) It was not uncommon to see desecrated Vietnamese bodies with folded cards tucked into their mouths. Grandpa was disgusted with the Vietcong's tactics but unlike the other soldiers, he did not agree with America's use of psychological warfare.

The heightened levels of danger affected the ways in which soldiers interacted, especially the African Americans who were disproportionately placed on the front lines. The higher ups thought black people were "better equipped" to deal with hostile environment of the jungle. The soldiers, reluctant to even learn each other's names, resisted building long-lasting relationships. Grandpa's closest friendships revolved around his role as an army door gunner/co-pilot of an elite helicopter crew.

Race played a large factor in his selection for the most dangerous position in the crew. His precision kills and lively personality are the reasons he remained on the squad. Grandpa came up with the nickname the Flyest Aces because of the spades and skulls painted onto the sides of the AH-1G choppers.

The Flyest Aces' unorthodox combat methods

earned them the reputation of being cocky and competitive daredevils. They compared their aerial victories to those of the other military branches. Some ill feelings had festered because of the lack of recognition door gunners received in comparison to Air Force pilots. The Flyest Aces quietly rooted for Grandpa to be acknowledged as a Flying Ace after his seventh victory. (A flying ace is an aviator credited with shooting down at least five or more combatants.) Grandpa kept up his spirits despite never receiving the Flying Ace designation. "We're the best out there whether they give us recognition or not," Grandpa said on occasion.

Grandpa learned to cope with the unfathomable horrors of war but one death hit harder than all the rest. He had no idea that Grandma was pregnant when he left for war. He received a letter from my Great-Aunt Josephine, "Aunt Jo" informing him of my grandmother's death. My grandmother hemorrhaged too much blood after giving birth to my father. The doctors did everything possible to save her life to no avail. Aunt Jo promised to take care of the baby boy until her brother returned home from duty. Grandpa couldn't fall apart, not now, not when others were depending on him on the battlefield. The only alternative was to suppress his feelings and to use the war as an outlet for his grief.

A year later, one of the Flyest Aces' helicopters was shot down in a firefight over the city of Da Nang. The crew parachuted out of the tail-spinning chopper and braced for a turbulent landing. The Vietcong pulled Grandpa and his friends out of the wreckage, stripped them of their equipment and threw them in a muddy prison camp.

The Flyest Aces suffered broken bones, bruises

and concussions. Grandpa was the only Ace not to wake up when they reached the prison camp. "Phil! Phil! Wake up! Oh no, he's not getting up. Somebody call the prison doctor!" The men shouted for the guards who were too busy taking their afternoon naps. A disoriented guard made the rounds and finally made the call to get Grandpa medical attention.

The guards rushed Grandpa to a military hospital where he was treated for his concussion. The doctors used the separation to try and drive a wedge between him and the team. Grandpa withstood weeks of "reeducation" for the sake of his country. The prison commander sentenced him to a month in a pit for insubordination.

The living conditions at the camp were terrible. A group of 8 prisoners had to share a tiny bowl of rice for days. The alternative cuisines consisted of the snakes or insects that infested the prison grounds. After a month in the pit, Grandpa contracted dysentery and lost a significant amount of weight from the infection. The crew's pilot, Mark Mitchel, spent close to a week alongside him in the pit.

"My ribs—they're showing. Oh my God. I'm going to die in this filthy pit and never hold my baby," Grandpa said.

"We've survived in this dangerous prison for this long. Don't give up. Picture your boy growing up without a father. That should motivate you in your darkest hours," Mark replied.

"Promise me you'll watch over my boy if I don't make it out of this alive."

"It won't come down to that."

"Promise me."

"You--"

"Promise me."

"Yes, I promise. You know you're my brother and your family is my family."

The prison commander, who was nicknamed, "the Badger" grilled the Aces for strategic military information. "What were you targeting the day we shot you down?" He asked repeatedly. Grandpa and the Aces remained tightlipped in the face of their oppressors. As a result, the interrogators ramped up the torturous acts. The Badger loved to wrap parachute chords around the prisoner's appendages, cutting the circulation to his fingers and toes. The immeasurable pain they experienced can hardly be put into words.

Some time later, the Vietcong marched the prisoners along a 6-month trail to a camp in the north. Grandpa formulated a plan to facilitate his crew's escape. At the halfway point, he attempted to steal a guard's gun, creating a diversion.

The Flyest Aces saw an opening and fled into the dense foliage of the jungle. Unfortunately, Grandpa bore the punishment for leading the jailbreak. He was imprisoned at the Hanoi camp until the United States negotiated the release of POWs in February of 1974.

The transition back to civilian life was tough to say the least. Grandpa returned to a seemingly different life, or maybe it was he who had changed. He felt the Army's work had been permanently invalidated by the My Lai scandal. The newspapers painted the soldiers as heartless monsters. It was easy for the condemn them. They didn't have to deal with the paranoia—they weren't there. He wasn't excusing their actions; he just thought of the media as scavengers eager to publish the most sensational headlines.

The American people lost favor in a war that ultimately had no endgame. The soldiers didn't create the mission but they were the ones left to deal with the fallout. No one considered the horrors they were subjected to on a daily basis. You can make the legitimate argument that they should have handled it better. To be fair, a soldier must demonize his enemy to justify his actions. In a split-second they have to make life and death decisions that the rest of us have been spared from making. They took on the responsibility of defending the ideals that are intrinsic to the United States, or at least that is what they thought they were there to do.

Grandpa endangered his own well being for a country, which treated him, worse than a second-class citizen. He went to Vietnam, leaving his pregnant wife behind to free another country from communism when he in fact wasn't entirely "free." To top it off, he now had to deal with being an unemployed, single-father.

He doubted his ability to be a stable parent and good role model for his son. Grandpa barely slept from fear of night terrors. Every loud noise put him on edge and Grandpa worried what he might do in a fit of rage. The flashbacks were so intense that he could even smell the napalm and hear the muffled screams. He vividly envisioned lost friends who sacrificed their lives, losing the ability to reach their full potential.

Grandpa's feelings were not easy to talk about with anyone, not even with Aunt Jo. He isolated himself from even the closest of his friends. Grandpa missed the camaraderie of being part of a unit with singular goals and clear mission objective. His platoon was filled with guys who dealt with similar issues. The threat of death superseded the racial divide that existed in the America. The bonds they formed were stronger than prejudice. The guys cared more about the heart of the guy next to him than the color of his skin. Grandpa returned to a country, which had achieved considerably less progress in comparison.

Drinking alcohol became necessary to calm the nerves and numb the emotions. The alcohol created as many problems as it supposedly cured. It magnified the feelings of alienation and caused him to plunge into a bottomless pit of depression. He lost touch with his own humanity and withdrew further from society. Now to feel anything at all, he engaged in riskier and riskier activities. Eventually, Grandpa found more constructive ways to occupy his time. He found work doing odd jobs for small businesses at less than minimum wage.

Grandpa learned of substantial payouts coming out of Atlantic City. He had become a skilled poker player while in Vietnam and decided to test his luck in New Jersey. The cash came fast and Aunt Jo feared the source of all this unknown revenue. Grandpa and Aunt Jo had a spat one night and they both decided it would be better if he moved out. Aunt Jo made it clear; she did not want her nephew to leave. She raised my father for the first few years of his life and she had been the only mother he ever knew. Grandpa was a troubled man and she saw the transformation he'd gone through. Aunt Jo wished there was a solution to help her younger brother.

Grandpa ended up moving into a rundown one-bedroom apartment. He just needed a roof over his son's head. That's when Grandpa realized how much his sister helped him. He wasn't able to stay out late or go to the racetrack alone anymore. Grandpa dragged Dad to the track twice a week for months. Luckily, a legitimate employment prospect came along and a company hired Grandpa to clean offices downtown. It was a simple job, which could have opened doors down the line. Grandpa had been doing well for a while until an inexplicable firing. He tried to get a straight answer from his boss but he wouldn't explain why.

This situation discouraged a man who'd been trying to right his wrongs for so long. It was back to the casinos every night and the racetracks every weekend. Word spread around town about a new casino named High Rollers Casino opening in South Philly. The High Rollers Casino employed attractive staff to work there every night. Their waitresses flirted with the customers and used their sex appeal to extract bigger tips from their wallets. This new casino turned into the place to be in the city. The rich right down to the commonest of man were frequent visitors. The local economy even benefited from increased traffic. Grandpa became a regular fixture at High Rollers. Everyone knew him there.

CHAPTER 4

BETRAYAL

Grandpa got on an amazing roll one particular Friday night at the High Rollers Casino. He won big against a collection of the city's best poker players. Grandpa received an invitation to the casino owner's private office for an impromptu meeting. The security guards escorted him into an elevator that led up to the second floor. They opened the door and offered Grandpa a seat in front of a mahogany desk. The men left the dimly lit office and stood guard outside the room.

Across the desk sat a sharply dressed olive-skinned man. Arrogance oozed out of the pores of his skin. "Let me introduce myself; my name is Vittorio Marco Rinaldi. You can call me Victor. I am the owner of the High Rollers Casino and you are here because some of your activities have caught my eye, Mr. Baxter. I am part of an organization, which is in need of services. Services I am confident you can provide. I see something special in you. You have talent, and I can use that."

"Much appreciation for the consideration Mr. Rinaldi, but I am just a nobody. I have no business being here. How could I be of assistance to an organization such as yours?"

Victor slid open the left top drawer and retrieved a small case. He unclasped it and selected two of his finest Cuban cigars. Victor walked around the desk and handed Grandpa a cigar. This gesture went a long way to calm Grandpa's nerves.

Victor had been keeping tabs on my Grandfather for an unspecified amount of time. He was aware of Grandpa's military service and more importantly, aware of his financial predicament. The profile of an indebted, disturbed, ex-soldier fit compatibly with his current needs. Victor pitched a mutually beneficial proposition. He offered Grandpa the role of his personal "cleanup guy." Victor required a trained gunman to eliminate his enemies without arising suspicion. To run a legitimate empire someday, Victor's hands had to remain clean.

Grandpa had his fair share of issues but he wasn't a cold-blooded murderer. He took lives in the past, but this was not the same. He killed because his nation asked him to, and being a mercenary would cheapen his military service. Victor sensed the apprehension in Grandpa's raspy voice. He explained that the job would pay better than he could imagine. Victor believed that Grandpa would've surely walked out of the room. The fact that he hadn't was a good sign. The offer tempted Grandpa after everything he had been through. He found himself in a unique position to make real money for the first time in his life. I guess the offer was too good to pass up.

"Weren't you a part of the Flying Spades or something?" Grandpa had been called a spade several times in the past and took exception to the casual use of the term.

"You're from Chicago, right?" Grandpa asserted.

"Yes, yes I am. Why does that matter?" Victor replied.

"It matters because Chicago mobsters committed unprovoked crimes against blacks during the riots and the police turned a blind eye. My cousin lived in Chicago, he told me stories about people like you. You and your cronies are not about to sit back and profit from my degradation."

Victor apologized for the perceived insult.

"Hold on, please sit back down. Here me out Mr. Baxter before you write me off. I admit that I used inarticulate language; it wasn't my intention to insult you or your race for that matter. I've always been fascinated with anything card related, especially aces. Do you know what the ace of spade represents?"

"My buddies in Vietnam used them to scare those little men. I think it represents death."

"You are correct about that, it does represent death. As a young child my father taught me the meaning behind card symbols. The original ace symbol was a "1" and not an "A". It was the lowest valued card. The ace is versatile. Depending on the situation it can either be the highest or lowest valued card." Victor used this not so subtle analogy to draw the parallels between the history of the card and the aspirations of my grandfather.

Victor's father, Jimmy "The Hand" Rinaldi had been one of the most notorious criminals of the twentieth century and is widely associated with the ace of spades. He came to the states from Naples, at the age of 21 with nothing except for the clothes on his back. The acclimation process was smooth as Jimmy established himself in Chicago's "Little Italy" as a brash and bold newcomer. He grabbed the reigns of leadership from a group of equally ambitious young Italians. His gang effectively used black hand extortion tactics to gain control of the South Side. They specialized in extorting money from the wealthy through the use of threatening letters. The repercussions were devastating for those who chose not to be squeezed. The gang bombed their shops or the owners and their families turned up dead.

Victor grew up idolizing the gangster lifestyle. He wanted his own mafia and the mystique that came along with it. He'd been fascinated by the clothes, money and women he saw parading in and out of the house as a child. During this time period, the men would never leave their homes without their shoes shined and a crisp double-breasted jacket. Chivalry had not met its untimely death, and even the criminals held deeply religious beliefs. The gangsters hurt people, but the women and children were off limits according to the gangster code of morality.

Jimmy's overconfidence manifested itself through provocative behaviors and pricey purchases. Vaunted by his ruthless and headstrong personality, he couldn't help but advertise his work. Anyone eliminated had been found with the ace of spade placed between the pinky and ring fingers. The visual of a cold lifeless hand holding a card became synonymous with organized crime.

As Jimmy's power grew so did the animosity from the would-be crime bosses. He grew bolder by the day, angering those who stayed under the radar. The police commissioner became obsessed with taking down the mob. He targeted Jimmy specifically and even had his picture on the station's bulletin board.

Organized crime had moved away from explicit forms of extortion and citizens demanded more from law enforcement. The gangsters smartened up and got involved in more indirect forms of racketeering.

The gang chose Jimmy's closest confidant and underboss, Ralph "Speak Easy" Caruso as the mouthpiece to voice their concerns. Ralph wondered whether he was the right man to deliver the warning to his stubborn friend.

Ralph invited Jimmy out to their favorite speakeasy, The Upper Room for a sit-down. The men traded stories at the bar and entertained the dames. Ralph made a last ditch effort to reason with Jimmy.

"You gotta stop showin' off, Jimmy. There are much smarter racquets out there to get into. You're on top and everybody knows it."

"Why are you being a mook all of a sudden, Ralph? I'm successful because of my methods and I refuse to change them for anybody. We're seriously talking business when we should be taking home one of the beautiful broads in here."

"You're gonna to regret not listening to me, I promise you. And when that happens, you can only blame yourself for what happens next."

Ralph delivered the concerns of the other men but couldn't get through to Jimmy. The rejection left a nasty taste in Ralph's mouth. He signaled for the bartender to bring another round of drinks. Ralph planned for this unfortunate outcome and paid the bartender to poison Jimmy's glass in the likelihood that his efforts failed to sway his friend. They toasted ironically to good health and good fortune. Jimmy rose the glass up to his face, evaluated it, but not a drop touched his lip.

"You're not trying to whack me are ya?" Jimmy

asked, as he chuckled. Ralph's heart raced, his eyes followed Jimmy's every move until he downed the whiskey. Seconds later, he collapsed in the middle of the tavern, startling the onlookers. The poisoned glass remained firmly grasped in his hand even after the impact of hitting the floor. Ralph reached into his pocket, pulled out an ace card and inserted it into the glass. He then stepped over the body, paid both their tabs and walked out of the bar without anyone daring to say a word. The usage of the ace card was a sign of disrespect that would not go un-avenged.

Young Victor had been ostracized as the son of an assassinated mob boss. He worked as a low level associate of a crime syndicate who aspired to have a leadership role. One of the first things Victor did when he started out was to choose an alias. He chose "The Brain", to convey a clear distinction between him and his father. A hand does not think; it acts as an extension of the brain. A brain processes, analyzes and controls the movement of the body. Victor learned through example to be more discerning than his father had been.

Victor's organization is known as the Black Hand Syndicate and it has been closely tied to the CIA since the early 1960s. Since its inception, the CIA had been running a secret training program for the world's greatest assassins. They used the assassins to dispose of dictators and established puppet governments through rigged elections. The Black Hand also had connections to the Soviets, which put them in direct opposition to the president at the time, John F. Kennedy.

The high-ranking officials of the CIA perceived President Kennedy's administration as a threat to their power. JFK intended on scaling back the size of the agency. He openly voiced his displeasure with clandestine operations both home and abroad. Robert Kennedy, the Attorney General of the Justice Department and younger brother of the president, shrugged off serious threats for years. He had risen in national prominence by opposing corruption and enacting the toughest anti-organized crimes laws to date.

In Dallas, on the night before President Kennedy's death, the CIA organized a meeting attended by Russian officials, mafia kingpins, and the labor leaders. They hatched a plan to assassinate the president, changing the fabric of American history forever.

The Black Hand Syndicate figured that their unholy alliance could be more powerful than actual governments bound by laws and regulations. The successful assassination of a sitting U.S. president was an impressive opening act.

After years of success, the Black Hand planned to branch out into non-political economic espionage. They were forced to launch this new program without the full resources of the CIA. The agency was under investigation by the Senate Church Committee after its illegal assassinations and coups came to light. The media attention pressured the CIA to publically terminate several programs and to move them to "Black Ops."

Victor offered his casino as the base of operations for the new program. He built High Rollers as a front for his heroin trafficking and money laundering businesses. Victor saw an opportunity to showcase his worth and made the best out of a bad situation.

A CIA profiler sent Victor the records of former

soldiers living in his immediate area. He read dozens of psychological profiles and only one candidate had the potential to pilot his mercenary program. In this candidate, Victor found a kindred spirit, a crumb that had also been at the mercy of life's pitfalls. Likewise, this candidate only needed someone to take a chance on him. After meeting my grandfather, Victor reaffirmed his decision to build this new program around him. He offered Grandpa the one thing no one else could—power.

"Governments are supposed to work for the people, not the other way around. The late John F. Kennedy, asked you to do for your country and you went out and fought his war. The only presidents I follow are on a dollar bill. You're supposed to risk your life out of a sense of duty and patriotism. Why aren't you allowed to expect anything in return? Now you're messed up and can't find a job to support your family. I am offering you the chance to be a power player, to sit at the big boy table for once. The pursuit of happiness is not an entitlement of the rich. It's a God-given birthright of every American. You shouldn't be confined to poverty, and now, you have an out. I can only present you the key, you must do the rest."

"I only stayed because your words ring true. You see the world for what it is and not for what it should be. Maybe that's been my problem. I've been doing the right things while everyone's been getting over on me," Grandpa replied.

Victor Rinaldi persuaded Grandpa to abandon his principles for the promise of champagne and limousines. What does it profit a man to gain the whole world and lose his soul? This is a two-thousand-year old question that is no less relevant today than the day it was proposed.

To fulfill the obligation to Victor, Grandpa had to attend the CIA's assassin training program in North Carolina. In North Carolina, he would receive specialized training usually reserved for elite operatives. Grandpa had only recently entered his son's life and felt conflicted about leaving during this delicate period. Grandpa didn't want to be gone for another 6 months to a year after making significant strides in their relationship. Once again, he'd been forced to rely on his older sister to raise his son while he was away. More importantly, it wasn't in his best interest to break an agreement with a mafia boss. If what Victor said was true—not going could've been detrimental to the safety of his family.

Grandpa begged Aunt Jo to let father stay with her for the next couple of months. "This is a great opportunity for me. I'll be getting my truck driving license and once I have it, I'll be able to care for Junior."

"I love Junior as if he were my own. But I don't think it's good for you to jump in and out of his life like this. He needs his father."

"Do this for me one last time, Jo. I promise I will send you lots of money. You won't have to spend a dime. The economy is in the toilet and the guys who didn't fight have a head start. This'll add stability for the first time since returning home from 'Nam."

Aunt Jo had always been a softie, unable to say no to her brother. She understood that he had lost a lot in the last few years. He lost his lover and best friend while he was across the world engaged in combat. Aunt Jo hoped he might return in a better mental state, capable of being a good father.

CHAPTER 5

GOOD MEN DIE

Ecclesiastes 7:15-18

I have seen everything during this senseless life of mine. I have seen good citizens die for doing the right thing, and I have seen criminals live to a ripe old age. So don't destroy yourself by being too good or acting too smart! Don't die before your time by being too evil or acting like a fool. Keep to the middle of the road. You can do this if you truly respect God. The New American Standard Bible

The CIA's covert operations are categorized under an umbrella organization known as the Special Activities Division (SAD). This division runs two types of operations, political and paramilitary. The paramilitary group, known as, the Special Operations Group (SOG), deals with the military operations that the U.S. cannot publicly authorize. This group collects intelligence, coordinates raids, and eliminates threats.

The Political Action Group handles the economic and political aspects of war. Grandpa was brought to Fort Bragg Special Warfare Center to train alongside of the non-official cover (NOC) (pronounced "knock") agents. NOC agents are the operatives placed in foreign countries to perform economic espionage. They assume high-level positions in American companies overseas. Few at these companies know the true identity of the NOC agents or their relationship to the CIA. These agents are without resources and diplomatic immunity, unlike the official cover agents, working in embassies.

To the unsuspecting world, Fort Bragg was the Special Forces base of the United States Army. In reality, it doubled as a Top Secret assassin school and research center of the CIA. Dozens of spies were trained there every year. Beneath the facility, the Political Action Group had the responsibility of developing the materials necessary to carryout covert missions.

Being at Fort Bragg was similar to living in an alternate universe where everyone happened to be highly trained and intelligent mercenaries. They recruited only the brightest minds to join their program. Grandpa's peers spoke multiple languages and graduated at the top of their classes. He stood out. Grandpa had no equal when it came to physical abilities though he lacked the capability to excel in the required fields. The individuals who populate this world are cunning and calculating, they do whatever it takes to achieve their objectives. Grandpa did not fit the bill.

The psychiatrists administered tests to assess the trainee's personality types. The researchers integrated decades of research to design physically and mentally demanding challenges. Recruits were expected to function after being deprived of sleep and working to the point of exhaustion. Many recruits floundered by exhibiting indecisiveness and doubt, a select few excelled. The ones who excelled under the intense training measures guaranteed field placement.

The cadets spent several months practicing combat formations in the woods of North Carolina. Early on, they assembled and disassembled firearms, disarmed bombs and practiced evacuation scenarios. The instructors ran shooting drills everyday to maintain peak proficiencies. A martial art expert named, Ichiro Kaito taught judo, karate and advanced countering techniques. The trainees graduated to constructing weapons out of common household items such as straws and rubber bands, making them formidable in any environment.

The Senior Instructor of the assassin program, Calvin Cane fought in WWII and had been a high ranking operative before his appointment to the instructor position. Special Agent Cane ran the administrative side while the training instructors managed the day-to-day functions. His hands-on approach often rubbed the training staff the wrong way. He micromanaged each aspect of the program and belittled their ideas.

In the training program, recruits were divided into 12-member squads. Each squad had a 3-member subgroup known as a fireteam. A fireteam is an infantry unit comprised of the strongest members of each squad. Delta Squad only had two members eligible for promotion, Ichiro Kaito, an expert hand-to-hand combatant and Alexander Petrov, a long-range marksman. Upon arrival, Grandpa joined the squad and filled the demand for a close-range gunslinger and pilot.

Delta Squad's diverse areas of expertise and mismatched personalities made them a well-rounded group, capable of handling a range of covert missions. Grandpa wasn't pleased to be working with an international motley crew willing to betray their native countries for the United States. As a former soldier, he understood the importance of patriotism and the reassurance from knowing that your teammates have your back.

The instructors assigned the bunks to correspond with the squad designation. They wanted the recruits to have awareness for the idiosyncratic traits of their squad members. The bonds they formed could've potentially saved lives or the outcomes of missions. Grandpa wasn't interested in getting to know his group members and shared his displeasure with Special Agent Cane.

"I came here to do individual work, not to team-up with these clowns. I served with real American heroes who risked their lives for this country. These guys, I don't know what they're after or who they're loyal to. I can't stare death in the eyes and watch my own back at the same damn time." He shared his feelings to the grizzled vet, who empathized with his feelings of apprehension. Special Agent Cane walked over to a file cabinet and pulled out some documents.

"What's this supposed to be? I don't follow." Grandpa read the front of the document and stated, "I've never heard of a Project MKULTRA."

"I think I can trust you so I'll let you in on some top-secret information. Petrov is a KGB defector and double agent. Years ago, the KGB murdered his friend who was a double agent for the FBI. Petrov's defection is predicated on self-preservation and the potential for revenge. Now, let's cover the Jap who handles the combat training. Our former agent, Lee Oswald befriended him during his stint in Japan. Oswald's endorsement of Kaito put him onto our radar. The more we investigated him, the more I was intrigued. We invited Kaito at the Atsugi Naval base, drugged him and transported him here to train our recruits."

"How do you know we can trust them?" Grandpa asked. "Alexander could very well be a spy sent here to infiltrate our government. This could be their way of taking us down from the inside. You know that's what they've always wanted, sir."

"Kaito and Petrov will not betray us because we won't let them. Project MKULTRA is a mind control research program. Don't you understand how it works around here? We get whatever we want because we control the world. You need to learn to accept that you're on the winning team and the referees are on our payroll."

The CIA's Scientific Intelligence Division ran classified programs in the 1950's with the goal of countering the biological weapon programs of the Nazis. The United States refused to allow the wealth of knowledge the Nazi researchers had amassed to fall into the hands of their enemies. The scientists were brought to America where they resumed their experiments under the advisement of the U.S. government. Operation ARTICHOKE was established to advance the known interrogation techniques of the day and to develop mind control drugs. Operation ARTICHOKE transitioned into the MKULTRA program where mind control and memory erasing machines were built.

After WWII, the U.S. initiated programs with the purpose of engineering biological weapons. Most of these biological agents were created with the purpose of decimating the black population. These scientists believed in eugenics and in their eyes the elimination of certain groups would lead to the birth of a genetically superior human race. Ironically, by the time Grandpa entered the program, those initiatives had already been "decommissioned" by President Nixon.

To generate the funds for their illicit covert operations and secret wars, the CIA emerged as one of the world's largest drug-running entities. The dirty money paid for coups in Asia, Latin America and the Middle East. Drug kingpins ran wild in South America, importing opium from places like Afghanistan without any resistance. The cartels flooded the United States with drugs, exploding in an epidemic.

Throughout the last century, the Black Hand Syndicate in accordance with the CIA, deployed mind controlled agents to foreign governments. The CIA sought out the best in their respective fields to be part of their mercenary squads, whether they liked it or not.

"I give you my word, kid. You can trust these men. When we are done they won't remember any of this. This is how our program survives."

"So I'll be grouped with a bunch of mind controlled stooges? I can't believe this trippy mind control stuff really works?"

"Yes it does and if you don't believe me by the end of your training, I'll eat my hat. I went against protocol, revealing this to you and now I need something in return."

"What is it?"

"I need you to go to a few sessions with the staff psychiatrist. I can't condone your erratic behavior or drinking. I can only graduate the recruits whose performance meets our highest standards."

Grandpa returned to his sleeping quarters and made an effort to socialize with his teammates. Ichiro welcomed the sudden change in Grandpa's attitude. They shared a bunk bed while Alexander slept in the single bed on the other side of the room. Alexander wasn't interested in having fun or making new friends either. He maintained a distance both physically and emotionally. Alexander only cared about completing the program and exacting his revenge on the Soviets.

That night, Grandpa couldn't catch a wink of sleep. He looked from the top bunk and found Ichiro deep in meditation.

"Do your demons keep you up as well?" Ichiro asked.

"Sleep has been a commodity to me for a long time. You want to talk demons? My demons have demons! What about you?"

"It's not my demons that keep me awake, I long to be with my family. I have a wife, a son and a daughter at home. I'm sure they are worried about me, by now they must think I am no longer living. Do you have a family waiting for you out there?"

"My wife died a long time ago but I do have my little boy. He's growing up so fast. One day I'm going to blink and he'll be a man."

Despite being raised in two entirely dissimilar worlds, the men found common ground on their shared experiences as fathers.

"May I ask you why you would voluntarily join this program? Is it the loss of your wife that drives you to self-destruction? I do not see you as a man devoid of morals like Alexander," Ichiro said.

"It's hard to explain my choices to someone who hasn't seen and heard the things I have. My time on this earth has taught me that I can't be as naïve as I once was. I'm not cut out for martyrdom like Dr. King or JFK. I've learned that good men die and the evil ones are granted the pleasures of this world. I no longer care for the riches of an afterlife. I'm taking what I deserve from now on."

"Do you truly believe the nonsense you're speaking? If so, you are destined to live a very long life, my friend."

The next morning, Grandpa reported to Dr. Livingston's office for his first counseling session. The door was open but no one was inside. Grandpa looked at a row of Dr. Livingston's family portraits as he waited for his arrival.

"Beautiful family, isn't it? I would like to think I had a small part in that," Dr. Livingston said.

"Oh, I didn't hear you come in. I was bored and looking at your pictures helped to pass the time. I must say I'm a little jealous, I've always wanted a big family."

"Usually it takes a lot more prodding for new clients to open up. You're making my job very easy for me."

Dr. Livingston apologized for the tardiness. His prior engagement ran over its allotted time. After briefly explaining the basics of therapy, Dr. Livingston discussed the results of the psychological evaluations. He found Grandpa's results on the Rorschach to be disturbing on many levels. Grandpa's answers on cards 8 and 9 reflected the trauma he'd endured in Vietnam.

"Mr. Baxter, you had some interesting results on

the your assessments. Can you tell me about the years you spent as a prisoner of war?"

"I didn't crack. They tested my resolve and I didn't crack." Grandpa's right leg jittered. He rested his hand on the thigh to calm the movement. "It was a more dangerous version of the Wild West, no riding off into the sunset, either."

"The terror of war compounded by the death of your wife must've been devastating."

"Her death robbed me of my recklessness, from that point on I had to be cautious. My son shouldn't lose both of his parents, I won't let it happen."

Following the second session, Dr. Livingston diagnosed Grandpa with traumatic war neurosis (pre PTSD diagnosis) and prescribed anti-depressant medication. Minutes into the third session, Grandpa sat noticeably relaxed because of the tone set by Dr. Livingston. He fostered an environment where open discussion was not only tolerated but it was embraced. It was nice having a stranger to talk to, someone who didn't carry the baggage of his other relationships. He suggested journal writing as a cathartic exercise to tap into some suppressed feelings. Although Grandpa objected to the idea of using a journal, he could not deny with the results. With the treatment issue getting resolved, Grandpa resumed the training.

The CIA's tradecrafts incorporate combat training, however the bulk of it has been based on avoiding conflict and averting detection. Under the Project MKULTRA program, the CIA enlisted the services of a famous stage magician named, John Mulholland to teach agents sleight of hand/misdirection tricks. Mulholland wrote two top-secret manuals, which the CIA used to gain a competitive edge on Russian counterintelligence. The manuals contained tips on how to slip someone a pill, pass covert signals or remove a document from a desk undetected.

For my 10th birthday, I received a magic kit in the mail from Japan. I mastered the card tricks and put on a show in the kitchen for friends and family. For about a week, I answered exclusively to the name, "Houdini." Was the magic kit a simple children's gift or a programing tool intended to implant skills without my knowledge?

The Research and Development team introduced a poison dart guns designed to produce undetectable kills. These guns shot frozen shellfish poison into the skin, mimicking the symptoms of a heart attack. Soon thereafter, foreign leaders mysteriously died of unexpected heart complications. The autopsies detected no traces of the poison and only a tiny red dot was left on the skin. The success of the poison dart gun created a demand for more undetectable weapons.

The final course, evasive and offensive driving illustrated maneuvers to escape dangerous car chases and carjacking. The program simulated situations where the recruits demonstrated their driving skills in populated streets, sometimes in broad daylight.

Grandpa and his squad completed the final training and were awarded their first official field mission in Angola, Africa. Delta Squad joined of the ranks with the Angolan Task Force as part of a convert operation.

CHAPTER 6

UN-CIVIL WAR

By 1975, the continent of Africa had become the center of the long standing Cold War between Russia and the United States. Both countries exploited the instability of Angola, which had achieved its independence from Portugal the previous year. The People's Movement for the Liberation of Angola (MPLA) and the National Union for the Total Independence of Angola (UNITA) formed as liberation movements. With independence reached, they battled to fill the power vacuum.

The civil war ravished the nation, destroying the economy in the process. The ruling faction, the MPLA had support from Cuba and Russia, forcing the U.S. to back the rebel UNITA. Angola's third faction, the National Front for the Liberation of Angola (FNLA), hired hundreds of foreign mercenaries in its quest for control of the government.

President Ford commissioned Operation IA feature, a covert operation to overthrow the new government. Delta Squad's selection for this mission hinged upon the makeup of its team members. The squad featured a secret weapon—a Russian double agent.

Grandpa piloted an aircraft to the southern African nation in August of 1975. The group jumped right into the middle of the action, helping the UNITA score sporadic victories. Alexander impersonated Russian operatives and tricked the MPLA fighters into carefully orchestrated ambushes. When not impersonating military, Alexander participated in raids and attacked convoys. Grandpa's fluent command of the Portuguese language granted the U.S. another tactical advantage. He infiltrated the MPLA's bases posing as a soldier and collected actionable intelligence.

In his downtime, Grandpa explored the rich cultural landscape of Angola. The influence of colonialism on the tribal customs created a fascinating ethnic mosaic. The diverse people who inhabited the nation continued to practice their traditions in addition to the beliefs the Europeans had imposed upon them.

Grandpa once observed a dance/fighting ritual known as engolo. It is a right of passage where the victor receives a bride. The young men who participated unleashed a wide array of spinning kicks, dodges and leg sweeps.

Grandpa communicated what he had learned to the Angolan Task Force. Alexander thought Grandpa's sightseeing expeditions weakened his convictions.

The small divisions, which formed within the group, mired the Angolan Task Force's success. It began after Special Agent Cane handpicked Grandpa to lead the squad. Alexander was livid. He perceived slight on the part of the administration. A Russian leading an American covert operation in the height of the Cold War would have raised eyebrows. The group dynamic suffered from infighting and jealousy. Alexander's stellar performance in Angola caused the rift to expand, undermining Grandpa's leadership.

Grandpa threw a poker tournament to relieve some of the animosity. He chose a cool night around a fire to bring out the cards. For a moment, the men seemed to have set aside their differences over drinks. Alexander promised to be on his best behavior but he couldn't help himself. In the middle of a card game he brought up Angolan politics. He mocked the plight of the people, knowing it rubbed Grandpa the wrong way.

"These people wanted independence just so they could fight amongst themselves. This is why the continent needs to be controlled. I know you don't agree. How could you? You are here connecting with your African roots."

"You're really bringing this up, right now? It won't help you to win this poker game."

"I don't need tricks to win, I am merely speaking the truth. The people are just as dependent as they were before. Now they are the pawns of Mother Russia and the United States instead of the Portuguese." Alexander had the unique skill of getting under Grandpa's skin.

Grandpa brushed the miniature card table aside and the two men went blow for blow. It took all ten men to break up the fight.

"I am going to kill as many civilians as possible. You thought I was bad before, wait until tomorrow. The blood of the innocent will be on your hands," Alexander shouted.

"Admit it, you're jealous. It's so obvious to everyone around here. If you kill one innocent person, I'll put a bullet into your skull, myself."

The argument deepened the fractured loyalties of the men, with everyone picking their sides. Although

Ichiro chose Grandpa's side, he attempted to mediate the situation.

"You have to be the mature one. Prove to the team why you're the leader and he's not."

"It's funny, I recall our conversation in North Carolina. Everything has transpired exactly how I said it would. Look what's happened here. How many freedom fighters have we killed while mercenary thugs are allowed to live?"

"You can't look at life that way. Certain things can't be measured under such simple criteria. The universe will take care of bad people when it's their time."

"It's never their time."

"Be patient, my friend."

On a routine reconnaissance mission in Luanda, Alexander veered off from the group. Grandpa found his vehicle parked a half-mile back, outside of a primary school ran by the Cubans.

"Are there kids in there, you bastard?"

"I think you know the answer to your own question. I'm a man of my word and I told you I would kill innocents."

"What's your angle? Thought you were above childish acts of revenge."

"I planted a landmine somewhere on the grounds. School is letting out in about two minutes. I advise you to find some cover."

Without hesitation, Grandpa fired straight at Alexander's head. The bullet grazed the side of his temple, right above the left ear.

"You shot me?"

"No. I nicked you. If I had the desire to kill you...you'd be dead."

The gunshot coincided with an exodus from the school. A fearful child bolted outside the building, triggering the anti personnel landmine. The landmine eviscerated the young boy's leg; blood and shrapnel flew everywhere. The rest of the children screamed in horror at the scene. Alexander escaped in weasel-like fashion.

Impaled by shrapnel, Grandpa staggered back to his truck. He reversed it as close to school as possible. Grandpa attempted to load the boy on to the truck but the boy's teacher blocked him. The Angolans had absolutely zero reasons to trust him. Grandpa fought for the rebel movement and his partner maimed a small child. "I'm trying to save this boy's life. There's still hope if I can make it to my camp."

Grandpa's sincerity must've shown through. The teacher helped him to mount the boy onto the truck. The teacher performed basic first aid until they reached the base.

Alexander ditched the Angola Task Force and joined the FNLA's ragtag mercenary team led by Costas Georgiou, a Greek mercenary. Georgiou was a psychopathic ex-soldier who aligned himself with the

Brits. He burned countless villages and murdered hundred of civilians. In 1976, Cuban troops captured Georgiou's team. They were tried in Luanda's court and sentenced to death for their vicious crimes.

Grandpa returned to the High Rollers Casino for the first time in over a year. Contact with Victor had been restricted so he was unaware of the developments of Project ATLAS.

In Grandpa's absence, Victor developed the logistics behind the newly sanctioned black ops program. The program, which Victor dubbed Project ATLAS, corresponded with the roles in the Sicilian Mafia's leadership. The capos (kings) are the bosses who hold political offices or run multibillion-dollar companies. These bosses remain in power through deception and intimidation. The consiglieries (queens) are the cocktail waitresses who work at the casino. The waitresses act as the middlemen, relaying information to relevant parties. The soldiers (aces) are the mercenaries who carry out assassinations. And a goner (jack) is the target.

Victor's business decisions were usually filtered through a nostalgic lens. He modeled the High Rollers Casino to resemble a 1920's jazz club. Victor mandated a strict dress code and hired live bands to play at the lounges. Ultimately, the transformation of High Rollers into a safe house benefited the NOC agents the most. They finally had a refuge to receive support and communicate vital intel.

A waitress showed Grandpa an unusual amount of interest. "Victor sent me to fill you in on the procedures of the Card System. At every safe house there is a "Regina" who acts as your handler. She is a "human dossier" who will brief you on mission specifics, target locations and evacuation options. Come in wearing a simple black suit, black tie and white shirt—not your groovy disco threads. Replace your pocket square with a numbered ace card to signal when you are ready for a mission. Once your mission is completed, remove the card and place it on the victim's body. When you are ready for a new mission, come in with a new card."

"Why does Victor care whether I wear a suit or not? It doesn't matter how I dress when I'm not in the field."

"The lounge's dress code was instituted to make things easier for you. A suit makes you blend in, that's why he said nothing flashy. Knowing Victor, he probably loved the symbolism. When you think about it, the only thing an ace wears is a suit."

They used the elements of a casino to conceal their illegal activities. Everyone knew and expected Phillip Baxter to be at High Rollers. Common sense dictated they keep up the imagery. The waitresses and live music distracted the guests from noticing the drop offs or exchanges. Payments were made in taxable casino winnings to keep the IRS off their trail. The CIA later set up Grandpa with a position at a truck driving company to explain his time at Fort Bragg. Victor had a contingency plan for every potential complication.

The ensuing years were kind to both men. They were able to make huge profits from their partnership. Grandpa cemented his status as one of this planet's elite mercenaries. ACE became a mythical figure in the criminal underground. The Rinaldi Empire expanded to Vegas, Tokyo, and Moscow etc. His main competitors vanished or quit the business. Grandpa's personal life suffered though. Even Aunt Jo stopped trying to reach her brother, believing he was too far-gone.

Dad was around 9 years old at this time and Grandpa had been ACE for almost two years. They no longer lived in the one-bedroom apartment. The mercenary wage paid for a condo where they now lived. Dad had a stable babysitter who stayed with him while Grandpa was completing missions. She had been a close family friend and Grandpa compensated her well. Grandpa actively hid his lifestyle, which wasn't easy. His sloppiness eventually led to the secret being blown.

Late one night, Grandpa opened the door to his bedroom and found Dad reading a huge chunk of his latest journal entry.

"How did your sneaky self get that book? I hid it where no one would look for it." Grandpa said as he angrily walked into the room. "You had no right to read my journal without permission."

"You kill people, Daddy? You're a bad man?"

"No, no, no. Daddy is sorta like the special police. I kill bad men but I can't tell anybody. You have to promise to keep Daddy's secret. I'm counting on you little guy. "

"Okay."

Grandpa knew he could not continue to raise his son in this environment. Over the next few years he traveled to South America, Europe and Asia for merc work. While conducting business in Japan, he called Ichiro and scheduled an appointment at his dojo.

Following the Angola mission, the CIA erased Ichiro's memories and disposed of him on a rice farm in Japan. A farmer stumbled upon his disheveled body and nursed him to back health.

"Thank you for penciling me in, Mr. Kaito. I know your time is valuable. I received word of your dojo from a business associate. I've been searching for a teacher to train my son and no one is more qualified than you."

"The agency taught you well, Phillip. You act as if you don't know me. The CIA used devices to make me forget our time at Fort Bragg. It didn't work. I remember everything we've been through together."

"How can this be? I've seen them wipe the brightest minds with regularity. Special Agent Cane was convinced that you were under his control."

"The agency did not account for my strong mind, reinforced by years of meditation. I have reached levels of consciousness, unattainable to most men."

"I'm actually happy that you remember me. I came here thinking I had to pretend we've never met. You're the only friend I have left and I need your help. My relationship with the CIA has me fearful for my son's safety. I think they'll use him to keep me in check."

"Your son needs a secure environment to grow up in and you are in no position to offer one. The CIA won't tamper with me again and run the risk of exposing their operations. I will train him for you. He will need to be strong to survive in our world."

Grandpa exhaled in relief once Ichiro agreed to care for his son. However, he did express concerns about Ichiro's Buddhist philosophies "infecting" his son's mind. Grandpa had given up on God and religions, altogether.

"I respect what you do. My only reservations are the Buddhist principals you live by. I am against the practice of religions. I don't think it's right to expose my son to this stuff."

"Buddhism is not a religion, it's a way of life. You love to gamble so why don't you take me up on a bet. Here are the conditions: If I train your son to be the greatest assassin alive, I am entitled to half the money you've earned from your mercenary work. If I am unsuccessful, the dojo is yours."

"That doesn't seem fair. You stand to lose a lot more than I do."

Ichiro's uncle fought and died in WWII and not unlike Vietnam, both sides employed inhumane and barbaric practices. The Japanese committed war crimes against their prisoners of war, which included Americans. To rile up the people, the U.S. government initiated an intense propaganda campaign. As a result, a number of American soldiers mutilated the dead bodies of Japanese soldiers. The soldiers' body parts were taken as trophies and the top prize was a human skull.

"You have to give me full control, that means no interference. I am going to turn your son into the ultimate assassin. I want to prove once and for all, the eastern methods are still the best."

Weeks later, Dad was taken to the airport, kicking

and screaming. The awkward pauses in their conversation spoke volumes. Their relationship had been strained by Grandpa's actions.

"Why don't you love me anymore, Daddy? I didn't tell anyone your secret."

"Why would you ask me that?"

"You keep leaving me and now you're sending me away."

"Son, I love you very much, that's why I am doing this. You may not understand this right now but one day you might."

Grandpa reached into his pocket and retrieved his Vietnam dog tags. He placed the tags around Dad's neck and kissed him on the forehead. He told him he loved him and apologized for his mistakes. Grandpa walked Dad to the gate and watched as the last piece of his humanity flew out of his life.

CHAPTER 7

FOREIGNER

Dad had never flown on a plane prior to this trip. He was seated with strange older people, going to a stranger place. It was tough for a child to be confined to a plane for over 10 hours. The flight attendants gave him special accommodations and made sure he was comfortable. Ichiro waited at the airport to greet the newcomer as soon as he touched down. Ichiro completely frightened him when they met. He didn't know this man from a random stranger on the street.

Dad looked to the right and to the left and saw Japanese people everywhere.

"Welcome to Japan. My name is Ichiro and you will be living with my family for the foreseeable future."

"Are you a killer, too?"

"I'm a teacher. I've taught a village worth of children your age. You can trust me, your father does."

"You didn't answer my question."

"I do whatever's necessary, even if it includes killing. I will teach you to do the same."

Ichiro bent over backwards trying to cheer up this new addition of his family, nothing worked. He was wise enough to know he couldn't force it. He needed to let the boy discover what Japan had to offer on his own.

Dad was given a tour of the traditional Japanese style home. He was first instructed to take off his shoes before entering. Ichiro showed him the living room and dining room, where the family spent most of their time. Next, he showed Dad the kitchen where Takara, his wife was preparing a meal. They went upstairs to the bedroom that Dad would come to share with his son, Kenzan. Ichiro left him alone to unpack. Dad was extremely bored within the first few hours. Ichiro's did not allow televisions in the home and the children, Kenzan and Sumie had not returned from school yet.

The children were so excited to have an American boy living with them. On the way home, they thought of bizarre questions to ask him.

"I heard that Americans are very rude," Sumie said.

"You're rude, are you American?" Kenzan replied.

"You're mean! I'm telling mom what you said!"

"Don't act like such a baby!"

"You're the real baby!"

Sumie giggled with excitement as soon as they reached the front door. The children greeted their mother then raced up the stairs to Kenzan's room. They were met with an unequal level of enthusiasm from their new housemate. Dad's standoffish behavior deflated the excitement the children felt.

Ichiro called the children downstairs for dinner. They washed up and prepared to eat Takara's meal. Dad noticed the low height of the table and the non-existent chairs. Kenzan invited Dad to sit with the family as they knelt in front the table to eat. Takara prepared a plate for my father as she did for everyone else. She wanted to make the meal special, something he'd always remember. She understood the importance of a good first impression.

Takara cooked rice that she served from a brown wooden bowel. Dad had eaten rice many times before but never this kind. The rice had been seasoned with wasabi that made it very spicy. My father did not like spicy food and usually avoided them. Takara forgot to mention the spiciness of the food. Luckily, Dad enjoyed it so much that he scraped the bowel. The tuna rolls were his favorite part of the second course.

The family skillfully used the chopsticks; it was harder than Dad assumed. He fumbled the chopsticks and Kenzan couldn't help but laugh. Sumie modeled the proper form for holding chopsticks. Kenzan helped Dad to finish eating the tuna rolls even though there had been friction earlier in the day. It took time before Dad handled chopsticks as naturally as he used silverware.

After dinner, the children prepared for bed. They had school in the morning and Ichiro hated tardiness. Before he fell asleep, Dad rolled over and apologized to Kenzan for the snarky attitude. Kenzan was relieved. He swore Dad hated him. The boys talked for hours about which teachers and students to avoid. Dad was grateful for the inside tips Kenzan provided. All of a sudden, Ichiro appeared in the doorway. The boys clammed up for fear of punishment. "Go to sleep, boys. Good night."

The next morning, the boys got dressed for school. Dad hated every piece of his new school uniform from the cheap tie to the shiny shoes. The first day was bad enough to overshadow the lousy uniform. He didn't understand a word his teachers said in half of his classes. His classmates heckled him for being the only African American child in the whole school. The teachers were strict and the work was more challenging. The school day started earlier and ended later than in America.

Kenzan and Dad sat together in the majority of their classes. Sumie was a year older and had her own social circle. After school, Sumie stayed behind to study at the library. The rest of her friends went with boys to play baseball on a small patch of land. The children left one by one, once it had gotten dark. Dad convinced the remaining kids to continue playing. When the boys got home the family had already eaten. Ichiro was frustrated with the total disregard of his rules. He was more upset at Kenzan because he knew better.

Ichiro sent the boys to sleep without dinner to teach them a lesson. Dad felt guilty for getting his new friend in trouble. Kenzan took it in stride, never complaining about the punishment. In the middle of the night Ichiro yanked Dad out of bed to address his immaturity.

"Psst…wake up, we need to talk," Ichiro whispered.

"Can we talk in the morning?" Dad replied.

"No. This cannot wait. Do I have to remind you why your father sent you here? He didn't send you here to sample the cuisine. You know the kind of work your father does for a living. You won't be kept out of it forever." Ichiro's words pierced in their condemnation. "You are

71

here to be trained. One day you will have to choose your own path. Until that day, you will do as you're told."

Dad reported to the dojo every day after school. Ichiro promised to provide intense training and did not take it lightly. In the dojo, Ichiro practiced a multi-layered form of training. Ichiro specialized in judo though he was an expert in various forms of martial arts from karate to aikido. His training emphasized the importance of strengthening one's timing and balance. Ichiro also noted how often people tend to overlook the importance of balance.

"You need to move your legs farther apart and turn your body as you strike. You're power does not come from your arms." Ichiro demonstrated simple and complex techniques to strengthen balance and increase dexterity. His methods were stripped down at first, which allowed his students time to mature and eventually flourish in his system. The lessons progressed at the pace warranted by the students' skill level. Sometimes, it required years for his pupils to advance in their studies.

Ichiro worked on improving instincts through sparring. He wanted students to be able to make the correct decision for each individual situation. He blindfolded his pupils and forced him or her to rely on the other senses. Dad learned to sense danger and negate it to gain an upper hand. Reaction time could be the difference between life and death or success and failure.

Dad studied his coursework on top of learning a second language. Every second of the day was structured to establish the discipline he lacked. A few weeks had passed from the beginning of training and Dad showed signs of improvement. He could not contain his excitement when he spoke to Grandpa on the phone. Grandpa did not expect such a positive reaction to being in Japan. In a matter of weeks, he had transformed into a confident young man.

Dad had been doing so well that Ichiro decided to reward his dedication. He planned a mystery outing for the Kaito family. He told the family to get dressed in their finest clothes; it would be a full day trip. Each child took a turn trying and failing to wrestle information out of Ichiro.

Ichiro fulfilled his dream of having his family experience his birthplace. He grew up in Kanagawa, a city located south of Tokyo. Kanagawa is a microcosm of Japan. Like the country, this area possesses a modern yet rich tradition. In this city, resides a historic theater that the family attended.

It took the family an hour for them to reach their destination. Takara announced to the children when they reached the Yokohama Theater. The children's eyes lit up when they heard the good news. Dad hadn't watched any television in months and this was the next best thing.

They entered the historic theater minutes to show time. The seats were in pretty good view of the stage. The lights dimmed and the show began. There were very few props visible on the stage except for backgrounds and trees. An eerie atmosphere was created through the use of chants and haunting music. Takara compared the play to a Broadway musical. The biggest departure is that men play both gender roles. The concept of men playing women blew the children's minds.

Ichiro sat next to Dad so he could translate the actors' dialogue. He briefly described the history of Noh theaters. "This play is practically identical to the version that was performed centuries ago. The story is about an emperor who received a vision in a dream. He was to have a special sword forged for him. The emperor tasked a sword smith with the burden of creating this sword. The sword smith worried that he was incapable of building it alone. He prayed to the god of his clan to help him complete his task. A spirit in the form of a little boy visited the sword smith. The spirit transformed into his true form and aided the sword smith in forging the magnificent sword. When he finished, the smith presented the sword to the emperor and the spirit returned to the mountain from which he came. This is one of the many age-old stories that have survived the centuries."

Even though every word wasn't understood the presentation kept my dad's attention. The actors dressed in elaborately embroidered and historically accurate costumes. Ichiro pointed out the large wooden masks the main characters wore. These mystical masks encapsulate the archetypes found in the Noh plays. Dad loved the animated expressions carved into the masks.

"The actors hold up the mask to their faces until they absorb the energy. Once the energy is absorbed, the actor may don the mask. The actor no longer exists only the character remains." Dad later noticed that some of the characters didn't wear masks. The characters without masks are known as, hitamen. The hitamen use their real faces to simulate a mask-like expression throughout their performance.

The children enjoyed the family outing very much. This had been the best Saturday night since moving to Tokyo. Before this trip, fun had consisted of any break from training. The exposure to the creative arts sparked my dad's imagination in ways nothing else had. Back at home the children discussed the fun they had at the play. Ichiro came to the door to quiet the boys down for bed. Dad sprinted to the door and wrapped himself around Ichiro's waste.

"Thank you Mr. Kaito so much! I'm going to work really hard from now on." Ichiro did not expect the warm reception.

Dad devoted the little leisure time he had, to learning about Japanese culture. Dad studied the shared history between the samurai and the ninja. Instead of playing cowboys and Indians, Dad and Kenzan played samurais and ninjas. Dad always picked ninjas because they could cheat and samurais couldn't. This newfound enthusiasm translated into a more focused student for Ichiro.

Dad idolized, Jim Kelly, the African American actor and martial artist. At a crucial stage of his life, he found an inspirational figure to look up to. Dad no longer viewed himself as alien or out of place for his interest in karate.

Dad begged Ichiro to teach him the moves from Kung Fu flicks.

"There's a movie where a brotha jumps onto the hood of a car and kicks the bad guy in the face. I want you to train me to be a cool ninja who's strong like a samurai."

Ichiro looked him straight in the face and said: "You do not know the meaning of true strength. The samurai valued honor and yet hired the ninja to do unspeakable things. True strength is not measured by force but in the willingness to stand on our principles. You won't understand 'til I teach you the art of the ninjutsu. Your first assignment: Read the *Art of War* by Sun Tzu."

Ichiro borrowed tactics initially created and mastered by the ancient ninjas of Japan. Ninjas did the dirty work of the samurai for centuries. Their honor code restricted what they were permitted to do. The samurai remained above the fray, not sacrificing their nobility while their underlings fought in parallel shadow wars. These ninjas had a level of financial desperation because of the limited class mobility in feudal Japan. Only those born into wealth could be samurais and the use of ninjas had been one way of distributing wealth to the lower class. Their indispensable services gained them notoriety among the upper class. Both sides of a conflict employed ninjas because of their merciless approach. They planted false documents and killed generals, tipping the scales of a battle.

The real danger of the ninja stemmed from their ability to blend into crowds. The movies love to depict the ninja in black robes and masks. Those outfits might sell video games and Halloween costumes but they're impractical. A ninja usually dressed in regular clothes in the course of a mission. The hallmark of a great ninja was to not arouse suspicion. The ninjas were masters of deception and played by their own set of rules. Ichiro envisioned Dad as the 20th ninja adept with the knowledge learned from centuries-old scrolls.

Ichiro felt it was his responsibility to guide my Dad towards an alternate path than the one Grandpa had traveled. He treated Dad no differently than one of his own. Years later, Dad realized the impact of Ichiro's teachings on his life. As a child, he craved the elusive father-son relationship. Ichiro taught Dad about life, love and manhood. He exemplified how a man should live and raise a family.

CHAPTER 8

GROWING PAINS

The years flew by as the children entered high school. By then, Dad no longer carried the same responsibilities around the home. Ichiro elevated Dad and Kenzan to the Assistant Instructor position. Teaching exposes how well an individual knows their craft. It requires patience, compassion and understanding. The boys had differing strengths when it came to the instruction of students. Kenzan was born to be a teacher. He watched his father do it since childhood. Dad withdrew from public speaking. The happenings at school inflicted damage

on his already shaky self-confidence.

My father dreaded attending the city's largest public high school. His peers made fun of him for being an outsider, a "gaijin." Once again, he had to prove himself to his fellow classmates. During the second week of school, a group of students heckled Dad in front of all the girls. The ridicule moved him down another rung on the adolescent social ladder.

The students were unaware of Dad's martial arts prowess. Had they known, they never would've singled him out. He exhibited a lot of self-control to resist the urge to handle things violently. By the third week, Sumie had witnessed enough. She scolded her peers, commanding the spotlight of the entire hallway.

"It's pathetic the amount of enjoyment you get from bullying him. Phil is a great guy who doesn't deserve this treatment. He's nice and funny and smart, he's everything you're not!"

The ringleaders left embarrassed from the chastisement by an underclassman. Dad was touched. He didn't expect her to run to his rescue. The news spread throughout the school and no other issues came up for the rest of the year.

In the aftermath of the bullying incident, Dad developed romantic feelings for Sumie. He debated the appropriateness of his first real crush. They shared a home. Sumie's family had become his family. Dad couldn't even tell Kenzan because of the touchiness of the subject. Dad called Grandpa for advice but he could not be reached. He was stationed in Latin America at the time.

Dad isolated at home and avoided Sumie at school. They were raised together; therefore, everyone in the home detected a change in his behavior. Kenzan brought up the subject on a day when Sumie stayed after school to study with her friends.

"You've been extra weird lately, not acting like yourself. It can't be ignored any longer. You know you can tell me anything."

"I'm just going to come out and say it. I got strong feelings for Sumie," Dad replied.

Kenzan, found himself unprepared for this type of admission. "You like her? I can't bring myself to think of my sister as a woman. On the bright side, you can officially become a member of the family." Kenzan gave Dad his stamp of approval to pursue a relationship, which meant a lot.

On Christmas Eve, Kenzan suggested a movie night at the local cinema. He invited both Dad and Sumie to hang out. An hour before the show, Kenzan informed them that he had to run a quick errand and would meet them at the theater. Dad and Sumie thought nothing of it and went to the movies. They waited in the lobby for twenty minutes. Sumie suggested they go find seats and save one for Kenzan. Dad chose aisle seats to make it easier for Kenzan to find them.

Dad and Sumie sat elbow to elbow for two hours. The scent of her perfume distracted him throughout the show.

The credits rolled…

"It's surprising that your brother didn't show up," Dad whispered.

"Yeah, it's not like him to bail on us. It must have been important for Kenzan to miss the movie," Sumie told him as they exited the theater.

They boarded a crowded train and couldn't even sit together. They reunited at the stop and headed to their residence. A light drizzle had progressed into a heavy downpour. Dad took off his jacket and covered Sumie with it. She thanked him and suggested they seek cover. They found refuge under a large building until the worst of the rain dissipated. Dad picked this moment to articulate his feelings. He uncharacteristically stumbled over his words.

"S-s-sumie, I've known you for a long time. Your

family has been like my family for the last few years. I had always looked at you like a sister until recently. I have these feeling that I can't explain."

She was reasonably surprised by his heartfelt confession. "I have feelings for you too, except my love is the love I have for a brother."

My father's pride did not accept her words. "I thought you were different from the rest of them. I guess I was wrong about you. Why would I ever love the foreigner?"

He left from the cover of the building and started walking home.

"Wait! Wait! It's still coming down," Sumie screamed as she ran after him. As they approached their home my father was unresponsive. This hurt Sumie; she didn't mean to break his heart.

Dad slammed the door to the bedroom.

"I'm guessing she rejected you," Kenzan said.

"I asked you not to get involved for a reason. You don't know everything. Stop acting like it."

"Sorry bro, I apologize. It's Christmas, I thought it would've been romantic in a movie kind of way."

At Christmas dinner, you could hear nothing except for slurping and chewing. Ichiro perceived a negative energy coming from the table. He told an anecdote to lighten up the mood. He reminded everyone of the first day my dad arrived.

"You didn't know how to use chop sticks. Every meal was an exercise in humility." Everyone at the table couldn't help but laugh. Kenzan tried to help you but he wasn't patient enough. You only improved when Sumie helped you."

Ichiro reminisced about the great times the family shared over those 5 years. Takara declared how proud she was of her children. She included my father in that sentiment. Their stories compelled Dad to make amends. He asked Sumie and Kenzan to meet him in the backyard. They sat in the yard looking up at the stars waiting for Dad to speak. He apologized to them and they happily put the mess behind them.

On Dad's 16th birthday, a special caller contacted the Kaito home. The caller asked Takara to keep the call a secret. When the children returned from school they were introduced to my grandfather. That was the first visit he made to the Kaito home since sending Dad to live with them.

"Wow, Junior you've grown so much. Got a little mustache growing now and got some bass in your voice."

Grandpa slapped on a happy face to mask the shame he felt. He missed countless milestones and desperately wanted to make this day special. Grandpa reserved a table at a nearby sushi bar and restaurant. At the restaurant, they discussed Ichiro's training methods in detail. From what he saw the mentoring had paid off. The one thing Grandpa did not appreciate was the change in Dad's personality. Dad had become all "peace and love" since finding inner peace. That was the exact thing Grandpa feared when he made the arrangement with Ichiro.

Dad went on and on about Ichiro and his great family. He had been introduced to a whole new philosophical perspective on life. Ichiro's family never tried to convert him to Buddhism though. They believed in people's right to make their own choices. Grandpa was visibly agitated by the direction of the conversation.

"Maybe, we can talk about you for a while," Dad suggested.

"You know I can't talk to anyone about my "activities." The less you know of my activities the better," Grandpa replied.

"What can we actually talk about, then? You treat me like an afterthought for years and now you show up and expect me to act like nothing's happened."

"Do you think this is easy for me to do? To look in your eyes knowing how much I failed you. The amount of blood on my hands is inconceivable. Do you really wanna hear about the families I ruined or the nations I've destroyed?

"No, that's not what I'm saying."

"Then what?"

"Did you even miss me, Dad?"

"How could you ask me that?" Grandpa replied.

"I just...I just never felt like you cared if I was around."

Tensions boiled over into the Kaito's home.

Grandpa and Ichiro had a heated exchange of words in the center of the living room. Grandpa ridiculed Ichiro's teachings and berated him for his lifestyle. Unnoticed, Dad watched the men argue from the top of the stairs. He respected Ichiro even more for how he handled things.

"You came to me Baxter, not the other way around. I haven't pushed my beliefs onto him. He's a young man in search of purpose and meaning. He would've come to you if you showed any interest in your son."

"You know better than anyone why I can't involve him in these things. He can't be weak or stupid. Where's the unstoppable killing machine you promised me?"

"How dare you question the quality of my work? Come to my dojo for a live demonstration. I will prove that you are not the best mercenary the Black Hand has to offer."

At the dojo, Ichiro hosted a private sparring match between Dad and Grandpa. To even the odds, Ichiro offered to blindfold my dad. Grandpa warned Ichiro not to disrespect him or his fighting ability. The time for the match drew near and Dad was conflicted. On one hand, he wanted to showoff the awesome skills he acquired. On the other hand, he had to go 1-on-1 with his own father.

Dad and Grandpa walked to the center of the tatami mat. Ichiro stood in the middle to recite the rules of the bout. A five-minute match with points awarded for knocking down the opponent or forcing him to tap. Both men agreed to the rules and Ichiro commenced the competition.

The men circled each other like vultures, neither wanted to make the first move. Then, Grandpa charged. Dad deflected the blow and countered with a throw. Before he could be mounted, Grandpa sprang to his feet and they exchanged jabs. Grandpa applied a grip hold and struck with a knee to the sternum. To break the hold, Dad initiated a one-armed shoulder throw into an arm bar. Grandpa writhed in pain, Dad applied more pressure to the left arm.

"Release his arm! Release his arm! You don't know what happened to it." Ichiro intervened, fearing Grandpa's pride would lead to permanent damage.

Grandpa had never seen such an impressive display of speed and strength. He conceded that Ichiro had won the bet "fair and square" and humbly apologized. He left a heavy envelope filled with cash. (Ichiro deposited the money into an account, which Dad accessed when he turned 18.)

He thanked Ichiro for equipping his son for future dangers. Ichiro cautioned him not to treat his son like a laboratory experiment. "He's not a Frankenstein monster and you're not the scientist. As much as you hate God, you sure do enjoy playing him. He's going to be his own man. Accept it."

Grandpa surmised that one day a wrong move or mistake would lead to his death. A mercenary, even the best of them is living on borrowed time. Before he departed, Grandpa had a very serious conversation with my dad. During this conversation, he admitted to succumbing to weakness when Grandma died. He removed his shirt and exposed a massive scar on his left shoulder.

"Look at this scar, there's still shrapnel lodged in there. It's nothing compared to the emotional scarring brought on by my guilt. In Vietnam, I witnessed a massacre and failed to act. Women and children were slaughtered like animals while I sat idly by and allowed it to happen. When a real opportunity to be a hero presented itself, I froze with uncertainty. Turning to alcohol was the easy thing for me to do. Please Son; don't grow up to be like me. A man is never going to be perfect but he does his best to do what's right."

It was an ironic statement coming from an unstable alcoholic mercenary. "It is too late for me, you still have a shot. Take it."

Grandpa returned to the states, picked up where he left off with another high profile assignment.

CHAPTER 9

BLOWBACK

In 1979, the country of Afghanistan achieved reform with the Democratic Republic of Afghanistan (DRA). It's new government pivoted away from traditional Islamic beliefs and leaned towards a more western perspective. An internal power struggle caused turmoil for the DRA, and Russia swooped in to prevent the fall of the regime. The Soviet invasion enlarged the divide between the less traditional government and the religious fundamentalists.

The United States played both sides of the conflict with the ultimate goal of running the Soviets out of Afghanistan. The U.S. supplied weapons to the mujahedeen faction, a terrorist group associated with Osama bin Laden. The terrorist group waged a holy war to rid the country of communism. American Muslims were trained for the mujahedeen faction and shipped to Pakistan. The CIA collaborated with Pakistan's Inter-Service Intelligence to arm the guerilla forces.

Grandpa was invited by the CIA to train radical Muslims at a Refugee Center in Brooklyn, NY. Initially, he passed on the training position for personal reasons. Grandpa needed a break to clear his mind. The CIA's leadership twisted his arm using an obscene amount of drug money to do it. Grandpa accepted the CIA's request and became an instructor at the center.

In December of '79, the National Security Council met in the situation room of the White House to discuss foreign policy. The president, the defense secretary and Special Agent Cane were all in attendance. Special Agent Cane suggested a surgical strike to counter the moves of the Soviets.

"Our government should use its trump card. ACE is the kind of guy who can grab victory out of the jaws of defeat. While he's there, ACE can also supervise the production of the opium. We're going to have to pay for this operation somehow." Special Agent Cane recommended Grandpa to lead a small rebel force, under disguise. "The Arabs can do the military's heavy lifting and absorb the brunt of the casualties."

Grandpa trained dozens of young radicals in the time preceding his deployment to Pakistan. He underwent an ideological indoctrination crash course to ensure the execution of an authentic cover. Grandpa grew a beard, wore prosthetics and had a false identity created for him. His cover identity, Ahmed Hammoud, was constructed within an hour of the meeting.

The next month, Grandpa reported to Jalozai refugee camp in Peshawar, Pakistan. He reconnected with his former trainer from Fort Bragg named, Ali Mohamed. His old friend Mohamed introduced him as an American-born Muslim and vouched for his credentials. They oversaw the harvesting of opium poppy to smuggle into the United States, filling the High Rollers' demand for heroin.

Grandpa confronted potential mistrust head-on and established himself as co-leader of the group. He spouted the rhetoric believably, galvanizing the support of the terrorist cell. Grandpa convinced the mujahedeen that he hated the ways of America. I wonder how much of it was genuine acting? Grandpa had reasons to resent the United States for their handling of the Vietnam War. He worked for CIA affiliated Black Hand but that organization served its own ambitions above all else. I fear the depths to which he sank to gain the trust of terrorists.

Grandpa and his team traveled to Afghanistan to battle the Soviets. At the camp, they met a young Osama bin Laden who appeared to be pro-American aid at the time. His family's wealth and influence made him an asset to the United States. Osama had been meek and incredibly soft-spoken for a man of such large stature. For that reason, the administration considered him to be their favorite "freedom fighter."

Grandpa and bin Laden crossed paths almost daily. He used those instances to pick the continuously spinning gears of bin Laden's mind. Grandpa and Mohamed saw potential in him to be a transformative leader.

Mohamed mentored bin Laden and trained him to utilize urban terrorism. He taught him the various strategic advantages of bombing populated areas. Bin Laden soaked in the teachings like an eager sponge. In the years following, he shouldered more of the load by running safe houses and establishing terror networks. Grandpa appreciated the extra time the added hands afforded him.

No one commanded more respect on the battlefield than my grandfather. He had practically two decades of combat experience and Special Forces training. Grandpa led an extremely successful campaign in Afghanistan. The mujahedeen pushed back the Soviet offensive using the familiarity with the mountain region and less sophisticated weapons. The Soviets were on their turf and the mujahedeen used home field advantage quite effectively.

One hazardous day, Grandpa and his team battled the Soviets along the countryside. A helicopter descended on them, cornering them in front of an abandoned farmhouse. They ran inside the house to escape the rain of ammo unleashed from above. The scent of napalm, the men strapped with bombs and helicopter fire oddly reminded Grandpa of something from his past. How could he have not seen it till now? America had re-enlisted him for a second Vietnam War except this time he was fighting on the other side.

This epiphany could not have happened at a worse time. Grandpa entered a catatonic state in the middle of the shootout. He refused to move; bullets zipped by his head, ricocheting feet from him. "Ahmed! You have to move, they are going to kill us all! Get up! Get up!" The terrorist cell managed to hold off the Soviet barrage long enough to escape the abandoned building.

The team lugged Grandpa's petrified body back to the base and out of harm's way. They offered him everything from water to women and still nothing. He burst out of the catatonic state within the hour.

"Why would they do this to me, again?" He repeated.

Victor called in a favor, requesting Grandpa's transfer to the states. He had a personal assignment, which he intended Grandpa to carryout. The dearth of command propelled bin Laden into an unfamiliar position as the de-facto leader. The torch had been unceremoniously passed to the next generation.

Two weeks had gone by since the transfer and Grandpa had not visited the High Rollers Casino. A night of excess prompted him to call his sponsor, Horace, in a drunken stupor. Horace darted over to Grandpa's place to check on him.

The front door was left unlocked and the house trashed. Grandpa was laid out on the bathroom floor. Horace cleaned him up and helped him over to the couch. Grandpa spoke candidly, for once, and disclosed details of stint in Afghanistan. Luckily, for him Horace thought he mistakenly referenced the wrong war.

"Why do you keep bringing up Afghanistan? You fought in Vietnam."

"Why did they do this to me? I can't get away from 'Nam, no matter how hard I try."

"It's over, it's been over. The news is stirring up the old feelings you've buried. Go to sleep and we'll pick this up in the morning."

Grandpa finally showed his face at the High Roller lounge a day later. He entered wearing a black suit, however he had not been wearing the ace card. Grandpa wasn't ready. A Regina crept over to his side of the room while serving drinks in the VIP section. He avoided eye contact with her as he grabbed a scotch at the bar. Regina put down the tray, moved behind the bar and initiated a conversation.

"You've fallen off the wagon?"

"Yes."

"We've been waiting for you to come back, ACE. Why aren't you wearing a card? Victor has an assignment for you, it's a really important one."

"I'm not ready... yet. Tell him to hire another one of the aces for the job. If it's that important then he should give the mission to someone in the right frame of mind."

"Victor trusts you, he says you're a standup guy. This job calls for the ACE not just any ace. This is a personal matter to him not business. The current jack is Ralph Caruso, the man who killed his father."

"Give me the details."

Grandpa knew how Victor felt about the murder of his father and couldn't refuse this request. That one event had shaped the way Victor conducted not only business but also his life. Grandpa flew to Chicago a day removed from the talk with Regina. He initiated the planning stages for the assassination as soon as he got there.

The Caruso family was under surveillance from the moment they woke 'til the time they went to bed. Grandpa mapped the schematics of the home, marking the placement of security cameras and studied the Caruso's sleeping patterns. Ralph lived in a fort and rarely left his home without a mini army. Ralph's list of enemies had grown considerably in the 40 years since he murdered Jimmy.

Ralph held a family dinner every Sunday at Antonio's Italian Restaurant. It was the only public place where he ever let his guard down. It was too obvious to make an attempt there. Grandpa sat in his car and studied the family's interactions through the front window of the restaurant. He watched the grandchildren having fun, enjoying their time with Ralph. Grandpa had forgotten what a relatively functional family looked like.

Grandpa turned on the engine as soon as Ralph walked out of the restaurant. Ralph's driver pulled out of the parking lot and stopped at the first light. Grandpa exited the parking lot as soon as there was a car between them. He tailed them from a distance of at least 100 feet until they entered his affluent neighborhood. Grandpa chose an unassuming spot across the street to stakeout for the rest of the night.

Grandpa used the layout of the house to avoid the cameras and subdue the security guards. He slipped in through the downstairs window, silently tiptoeing up the spiral staircase, down the hallway into the master bedroom. He stood at the foot of the bed observing Ralph and his wife in deep slumber. He chloroformed the wife first, pressing down, forcing her to inhale the chemical. Grandpa shifted focus to Ralph and chloroformed him as well. He sealed the windows and the door upon leaving the bedroom.

With the first phase complete, he implemented the cover up measures. Grandpa created a leak in the gas pipe, allowing the fumes to accumulate in the house for hours. He lit up a cigarette, inhaled twice, releasing the smoke through his nostrils. He flicked the cigarette and got far, far away to watch the fireworks.

The subsequent explosion rocked the neighborhood; emergency services arrived on the scene in near record time. The firefighters invested hours combing the wreckage for survivors and battling the flames. Some of the neighbors monitored the events from their windows. Others stood on the lawn investigating the disturbance. Once the fire had been extinguished, the paramedics emerged from a dark cloud of smoke carrying the charred remains of Mr. and Mrs. Caruso.

Because of Ralph's known mafia affiliations, an autopsy was performed. Midway through the examination the coroner found a white object stuffed down Ralph's throat. The coroner removed the remnants of a blood soaked playing card from his neck. The newspapers got ahold of the story and plastered it on their front pages. The message had been sent to the rest of the Mafia crime families. Victor Rinaldi and his associates should not be taken lightly.

Grandpa returned to the casino for his payment and received a boatload of casino winnings. ACE was back and better than ever.

Project ATLAS mandated Grandpa undergo another round of psychological evaluations to determine whether he was fit for duty. They scheduled the evaluation to be performed at a government building under the guise of veteran counseling. One of Project ATLAS' psychologists conducted the assessment.

"Can you tell me about your experience in the Middle East? In your file it says that it elicited memories you had suppressed."

"The dam broke and the buried memories rushed to the surface. The striking parallels to the wars, it broke me. I lost everything in Vietnam and I couldn't bear to live through the torture a second time."

"Where are you now…emotionally?"

"I've resolved those feelings. At this stage in my

life I have nothing to lose. I am committed to Project ATLAS, the Black Hand and the CIA."

"You've passed the psychological evaluation. I'm recommending your return to the field."

Victor transitioned from the distribution of heroin to cocaine. His supply of the purest cocaine on the east coast, garnered him a loyal customer base. He nicknamed his brand of crack cocaine, "Menace" because of its effect on the users. The Black Hand flooded the urban areas with crack, preying on the poor and downtrodden. The administration's hypocritical anti-drug campaigns stigmatized the victims of the international drug trade. Therefore, campaigning against the problem they had caused.

CHAPTER 10

MADE MEN

The mob wars that occurred in Philadelphia during the 1970s and 80s mirrored the brutality of any global conflict. The catalyst for the last bloody mafia war was the unsanctioned murder of Angelo Bruno, one of the last traditional godfathers.

As an adolescent, Angelo "The Gentle Don" Bruno emigrated from Sicily to the United States. He put down roots in Philadelphia where he formed close ties to an organized crime syndicate. Bruno's loyalty and shrewd business practices set him apart from those vying to move through the ranks. The Mafia leadership eventually promoted Bruno to the "boss" position of the Philadelphia crime family.

Bruno's comparatively non-violent approach kept him and the family out of prison and the papers. He restricted the men from trafficking drugs and endorsed the traditional rackets such as, loansharking and bookmaking. Bruno wasn't adverse to the other families trafficking in his neighborhoods though, as long as he shared in the profits.

The new generation of mobsters resented Bruno who had gotten rich and hindered their upward mobility. Bruno's conniving consigliere, Antonio "Tony Bananas" Caponigro, arranged an unsanctioned hit on the mafia boss.

On March 21, 1980, a hit man was dispatched to eliminate the Gentle Don. Angelo Bruno and his driver were parked outside his home when a gunman unloaded two slugs into the back of the head. The driver managed to survive the assault with only minor injuries.

The death of Angelo Bruno angered the Mafia leadership, collectively known as the Commission. The Commission is made up of the heads of the New York, Philadelphia and Chicago crime families. The majority of the power lied with the heads of the five New York families. Any perceived animosity between the families weakened all of them. Tony Caponigro violated omerta, the code of loyalty that separates the mob from the common criminal. For his transgressions, he had to pay.

A tear doused the morning paper as Victor read the cover story. He was awoken in the middle of the night with news of the execution. Even so, reading the particulars of the assassination in black and white print crystalized the reality of the loss.

Angelo Bruno was a surrogate father, who sponsored Victor's induction into the crime family. He took Victor under his wing and allowed him to be the only member of the family to traffic drugs. This sort of hypocrisy sat well with no one in the family.

Victor attended Bruno's funeral at Holy Cross Cemetery with his wife and two sons. He grieved amongst the thousands who came out to pay their respects. Victor vowed revenge as he leaned over the bronze casket. "I will punish the men who did this to you just like I avenged my father. These young punks don't respect the old ways. They don't respect the La Costa Nostra or the omerta anymore."

Victor called the Philly Regina into his office. "Regina, get in here, I have something that requires your attention." She entered the office and seductively unbuttoned the top button of her shirt. "Not that kind of meeting for once, babe. You've heard what happened to my mentor last week. When you see ACE let him know I have an assignment for him."

Regina spotted Grandpa feeding change into a slot machine.

"Victor is in bad, bad shape. I've never seen him like this...ever. His mentor, Mr. Bruno was killed last week. Victor's too prideful to come out and tell someone he's hurting. He's planning on going up against the Commission and he wants you to act as his driver when he does it."

"Victor must've sniffed out a traitor or why else would he do something this stupid?"

"No, from what I've been told Tony Bananas acted alone. He has some gigantic cajones to kill a seating member of the Commission without clearing it with the New York families. Victor wants a say in how the consequences are doled out and you're going to help him."

"I'm tired of fighting in these wars—domestic or foreign. A life without peace is not a life at all. "

"Think of it as you're providing backup just in case the Commission fails to look at things his way. Vic refuses to leave anything to chance."

"Victor and I have worked together for ages. I am quite knowledgeable about how he operates. "

"I didn't mean to imply--"

"It's fine. I shouldn't have taken out my frustrations on you. The Commission is the most powerful adversaries I've had to face and it's distressing."

The powerful stable of gangsters met in New York to discuss the situation in South Philly. Tony's actions were unacceptable and wouldn't be tolerated by any of the crime families. Victor barged into the deliberation room with Grandpa in tow. It was like a scene ripped out of a classic gangster movie.

"What is the meaning of this? You dare bring a moolie to our table." Chicago's godfather asked.

"I'm only here to claim the Philly seat for myself," Victor replied.

"The Commission has already decided to vacate the Philadelphia seat. Don't take it too personally. We're sympathetic to your grief. Bruno meant more to you than any of us could ever know."

Victor slowly looked over his right shoulder. "Hey, ACE. Where am I originally from?" Grandpa removed two pistols from his holsters and aimed at the Chicago godfather.

"You're from Chicago, sir." Grandpa answered.

"Hmmm…correct as usual, my good man," Victor replied. "I should vacate another seat if this one is unavailable."

Victor sat in the Philadelphia chair and kicked his feet up. He lit up a cigar as he said, "A seat has just opened up. Am I right? The position can be officially vacated but unofficially it's mine. Everyone at this table cared for Bruno. I'm not going to waste my breath disputing that. The family oath used to mean something. Losing our morality is the reason my father is not alive today. An example has to be made out of Tony "Bananas." My associate, ACE, will do the job unless anyone objects."

This act of bravado did not sit well with the members of the Commission. Unlike the senior members of the inner circle, Victor reeked of "new money" and because of that, the members of the Commission underestimated his business acumen and ruthless determination to succeed. It was smarter to appease him rather than to fight him outright as long as he kept his ego in check.

In April of 1980, the police found Tony Caponigro's dead body stuffed into the trunk of an abandoned car. The battered corpse was plugged up with cash on both ends to denote his greed. The co-conspirators were also murdered for their complicity in the assassination plot.

The next boss, Philip "Chicken Man" Testa also fell victim to an orchestrated hit. He was killed on his front porch by a nail bomb explosion. By then, the instability of the Philly Mob had been apparent to the other gangster families.

In an hour of desperation, Victor sought Grandpa's counsel on how to handle the dysfunction. "You guys ran together in Atlantic City from what I remember. What's your opinion on Nicky Scarfo?"

"He used to be my bookie before I joined your organization. Very cutthroat, suave and smart…a flashier version of yourself," Grandpa answered.

"You better be sure about this recommendation. This is my first big decision as part of the Commission. They're expecting me to appoint someone who can fix the chaos in Philly."

"I'm hesitant to give Scarfo a glowing recommendation. The power might go to his head."

"Name one person who hasn't been corrupted by power… I'll wait. The "gentle" approach has not worked. Maybe we ought to go in the opposite direction."

The Commission named Nicodemo Scarfo Sr. as

the successor of the slain boss Philip Testa. They promoted Scarfo who had been languishing in Atlantic City where Bruno banished him for being too violent.

Scarfo had a fondness for Chicago style gangsters. His brutal regime reflected Victor's views on the crime family going forward. "I loved Angelo's style but "Little Nicky" is a man after my own heart. The world has changed and we must adapt or die." The new don was literally the antithesis of the Gentle Don.

Predictably, Scarfo's tenure as boss was as disastrous as Jimmy Rinaldi's. The unnecessary killings brought unwanted attention to the Philadelphia family. Murders and arrest records multiplied and in 1988, Scarfo himself was convicted on RICO and murder charges.

The Commission hired Grandpa to whack Scarfo's son, Nicky Jr. "This organization has to sever all ties to the Scarfo family. With the father in prison, the only loose end out there is the "junior."

On October 31 1989, Nicky Scarfo Jr. was shot multiple times while dining at an Italian restaurant. Grandpa visited his table wearing a skull mask and holding a trick-or-treat bag. He pulled out an automatic pistol and fired. As fate would have it, Nicky survived the hit attempt. He got the memo and fled to New Jersey as soon as the doctors released him from the hospital.

CHAPTER 11

WHAT HAPPENED IN VEGAS?

In the late 80s, things gradually changed in the Kaito home as it did in Japan. Ichiro began to loosen the strict rules he insisted the family follow. More responsibility was placed on Kenzan, who was now the head instructor. Ichiro softened his stance on televisions and brought one home to the family. With a television in the home, Dad could finally catch the terribly dubbed action movies that played on the weekends. The only obstacle to his TV time was Sumie's sappy dramas.

"Sumie, I just want to watch one movie. You can have the TV for the rest of the day." Dad always had to bargain with Sumie to let him watch his favorite shows or he wouldn't get any time. "My favorite show is coming on in 5. I'll do your chores for the rest of the week."

"Mom won't let you do my chores because you're the furthest thing from a good cook."

"C'mon, I'm asking for two hours out of the whole day."

"Alright, just this once."

In those instances, Dad considered getting his own place. The Kaito family gave him so much over the years; the time had come to stand on his own two feet. He completed the apprenticeship Grandpa and Ichiro agreed on. He could not think of a credible reason to keep living in their home.

Dad and his friends loitered around the arcades every weekend. Their objective one Friday night was to devour their dinner and to enjoy the rest of the evening at the arcade. Japan had the best arcades in the world and teens competed against each other for the highest score. Dad and Kenzan were no exceptions.

Ichiro looked increasingly distracted at the dinner table. Takara snapped her fingers, bringing him back to earth. He apologized for the inattentiveness and pretended to listen to her ramble on for the duration of the meal.

After dinner, Ichiro asked Dad to join him in the meditation room for some tea. Kenzan was dressed and impatiently waited on him to go to the arcade. "Kenzan, go ahead I'll meet you at the arcade," he said. Ichiro prepared the tea for them to sip as they conversed.

"I have some terrible news to give to you."

"What is it? Should I sit down?" Dad replied.

"Yes, have a seat. You're aunt, she called the house this morning. She told me your father passed away, yesterday. Nobody knew Phillip had cancer. By the time he found out, the disease had already been in an advanced stage."

"Whoa, I'm...speechless...this surreal for me. I have to leave for America as soon as possible. I have to go back home to be with Aunt Jo."

On the day of his flight, my father articulated his plans to stay in America. Japan was an escape for him, he loved being there but he could no longer dodge his past. Dad gathered the family minus Ichiro in the living room to say his goodbyes.

He first addressed Kenzan. "Thank you for being the brother I never had. You know my history. I grew up mostly by myself and the transition into your family was rough. The whole process happened against my will. Now I can't imagine what my life would have developed if I hadn't come to Japan. I never told you how much I appreciate you for selflessly sharing your father's attention. At times, Ichiro neglected you because he was teaching at the dojo. I envied what you guys have. I'm still in awe of how you accepted the monumental changes to your life."

Then Dad thanked Sumie for her unwavering belief in social justice. He told her she should be a politician. "You risked your reputation for me, the outsider. For the guy who does not belong here and yet called it home. The world needs more people who are willing to stand up for what's right even when it's not easy." Dad assured Sumie that his departure had nothing to do with her. "I will always cherish your honesty and your big heart."

Lastly, he thanked Takara for being a wonderful second mother. Aunt Jo had been his only motherly figure until he moved to Japan. "Takara, this family would have fallen apart a long time ago without you. When my shirts were missing buttons you sewed them back on. When I grew older, you taught me how to do it. At night, we worked on my use of the Japanese language. You shared interesting stories of your childhood and gave me timely advice. Your warm and nurturing personality always makes me feel at ease."

Ichiro accompanied Dad to the airport. It brought symmetry to the whole experience. Ichiro accept no parting words from my father. He had a few choice words of his own though.

"I was supposed to be your teacher but you ended up teaching me about forgiveness. I expected you to be a spoiled American brat; you're the exact opposite of that. You remind me of myself, more accurately you remind me of who I used to be. Thank you for making me a better person." Ichiro turned away, glassy-eyed and full of emotion.

"You don't have to thank me for anything," Dad said.

"Yes, I do. I owe you plenty. This isn't a goodbye. I expect to see you again, son."

"You called me son?"

"I can't replace your father and I'd never try to. I'm here for you if you need me."

Dad taught him to open his heart to outsiders, something he never imagined possible. Ichiro irrationally judged an entire nation for the actions of a select group of soldiers from a past generation. The contempt for America had seeped into the other parts of his life, clouding his judgment. The inability to overcome his negative feelings deprived him of entering into a higher level of consciousness.

Dad surprised Aunt Jo at her home in southern Philadelphia. She looked as if she had seen a ghost walking through the front door. Dad left almost a decade earlier and had returned as a man six-foot tall, sporting broad shoulders. They caught up on the life developments over a hot meal. Aunt Jo gave Dad the keys to Grandpa's condo so he could have a place to stay.

The old neighborhood suffered mightily in the years he was gone. Grandpa's passing only added fuel to the fire of instability. The towns weren't safe, chaos and madness ruled in its truancy. The changes implemented by the new leadership within the Commission, had not produced the desired effects.

Grandpa was honored with a military funeral, which included a choreographed march and capped off by 21-gun salute. The Flyest Aces were among the guests in attendance. They paid their respects, one by one, speaking highly of Grandpa as a man and as a soldier. The ceremonial guards folded the American flag draped over the casket into a triangular shape. A guard marched down the aisle, knelt down and handed it to my father.

A grief-stricken Aunt Jo said, "I'm not feeling good. Touch my forehead I'm burning up." She rested her head on Dad's shoulder and collapsed.

A man pretending to be a ceremonial guard, pulled Dad aside and whispered, "You see the large bearded fella sitting over there behind your aunt? His name is "Ivan the Terrible" and he's not a nice guy. In his hand is what appears to be an umbrella. It's actually a mechanized pneumatic device that releases an airborne pathogen. You'll be attending another funeral next week if you disobey any orders I give you from here on out."

"Why are you doing this to us? We've done nothing to you."

"Junior, your father worked for the most powerful

men in the world. He left some unfinished business that you have the pleasure of finishing for him."

"Please, don't kill her, okay? What do you want from me?"

"Nothing, for now. When the time comes we'll find you. And don't worry about your aunt, she'll be fine after a few days of bed rest."

A few months had passed, and Dad still hadn't readjusted to living in western society. The music, the clothes, and the girls perplexed him. He needed to get out into the real world, meet new people. Kenzan talked Dad into visiting Fairmount Park, a place he had gone to many times with his aunt. The park had an abundance of history, art and culture. Dad stopped in front of a sculpture of a man spearing a lion on horseback. As a kid it towered over him, as an adult he truly appreciated the dynamic sculpture.

"This is a magnificent sculpture by Albert Wolff. It's actually the sister piece of the original, which is composed of limestone." The voice came from a captivating young lady.

"I see you know your art." My father was pleasantly surprised to make her acquaintance. "I'm no expert but I do know beauty when I see it. There is a lot of beauty in this park, especially today. The name's Phillip, by the way and you are?"

"Regina. It's nice to meet someone who appreciates fine art. We're a dying breed—you and I. Most people in America rather watch a music video nowadays."

"Are you an artist or do you come here to enjoy nature?"

"A little of both, I paint as a hobby. My dream is to be a teacher someday. Can I ask you a question? I don't want to be rude, you don't have to answer it if I cross a line."

"Ask away."

"Where are you from? You walk, talk and dress like no one I've met before."

"Well, I'm from Philly originally, but I've lived the better part of my life in Japan."

"That's fresh! I'm fascinated by Asian cultures. I've got to ask you some questions about your life in Japan."

"Maybe, we can talk about it over dinner or after a movie?"

They had an immediate connection that neither of them could explain. Dad's enigmatic vibe intrigued her and Regina made him feel normal again. Regina declined the date; she had to attend a class that night.

"There's this casino called the High Rollers where I like to hang out at. How about you meet me there around 8 o'clock on Saturday?"

"My dad used to go there all the time when I was a kid. It'll be cool to see what all the fuss is about."

On Saturday night, Dad arrived at High Rollers

excited for his date. He searched the casino floor for a half hour and did not see Regina anywhere. Dad couldn't believe she'd stood him up. The night didn't have to go to total waste he thought. He decided to stay for the jazz show in the lounge.

Dad chose an empty seat up close to the stage. A beautiful waitress offered him a drink and her company.

"Can I offer you something cold to drink, sir?"

"No thanks. I don't drink alcohol."

"Wow. You're nothing like your old man. You look more like the "menace type." It's very pure, not stepped on."

"How do you know who my fa--"

"Now presenting, the lovely, the incredible, the vivacious, Regina!" The announcer shouted the side of the stage.

A spotlight illuminated the dark stage, shining a light on Regina. She sashayed over to the ribbon microphone and belted out a sultry note. Dad's jaw dropped. He straightened his spine and perked up in his seat. Regina had on a black shimmery dress, showing off just enough leg. She sang a catalogue of bluesy numbers before leaving the stage. The crowd was in a frenzy screaming, "Encore! Encore! Encore!" She returned to the stage to do one last number.

Regina placed a chair in the center of the stage and pulled Dad out of the audience. She sat him down and danced around as she tossed her hair from side to side.

You could feel their chemistry emanating from the stage.

At the end of the performance, Regina showed Dad to her dressing room. She changed her clothes in the bathroom as they spoke.

"What's going on? Is this a date or something else?" Dad asked.

"I have to be honest with you. My real name is, Alicia Riche not Regina. My boss threatened to kill me if I didn't bring you here. I'm sorry."

"Who are you working for lady?

Alicia came out of the bathroom in a silk robe and slippers. "The Black Hand, the same guys your father worked for."

"I don't blame you for this situation. I've been waiting for them to make the call. A Russian man confronted me at my father's funeral a few months ago." Dad placed both of his hands on Alicia's shoulders. "Did you know my dad? A girl out there alluded to it."

"I didn't get to work with him exclusively. They recently promoted me to "Regina" status."

Alicia explained the Card System and her role in it. Project ATLAS had been paying her college tuition for years. She had been naïve to think that they wouldn't ask for anything in return. Desperation influenced her motives, her father's business had closed down and she had no other options.

Dad gave her a message to give to the Black Hand

leadership. For the ACE persona to work, he had to make it his own. On covert missions, he opted for a black hooded body suit made of neoprene and Kevlar. Dad had essentially become a ninja to the Black Hand's samurai both visually and functionally.

"You should hate me for this, I don't blame you if you do. I'm not the sort of person who takes part in these sort of illegal activities. The sad thing is I honestly do like you a lot. Unfortunately, the rules prohibit romantic affairs between queens and aces."

"I won't let them keep me from achieving true happiness. It's as if someone or something is trying to control my life at every turn. I'm my own man, whether people believe it not. I'll find a solution to our problem, even if it's the last thing I ever do."

"Maybe, we can keep this our little secret. We can spend time together at the lounge and sneak out whenever it's possible. If we're careful we won't get caught by our bosses."

"I want to be optimistic but these guys are always watching. We won't get away with this plan of yours."

"We have to try, the Black Hand has more important business to worry about than who you're dating."

The forbidden relationship progressed at a meteoric pace. The situation created a certain level of excitement. They snuck out from time to time to steal kisses in the backstage dressing room. Alicia rarely went for the bad boy type. As a young woman, she rebelled against anyone who sought to control her.

The day came to meet Alicia's "perfect" family, as Dad would put it. He dressed conservatively in something her father would approve of. Alicia's pulled up to the upper middle class home and parked in the driveway. They nervously waited in the car for an extra five minutes. She prepped Dad for the likely conversation and much more.

"You ready?"

"Nope, not ready yet. Give me another minute to pull myself together. Your pops is going to hate me."

"He's not as bad as I make him sound. Okay, maybe he is. He's not the type to pull back on his punches."

Alicia introduced her parents, Maurice and Kim Riche. The Riches were a devoutly religious family-oriented couple. They openly disapproved of the relationship. Their desire was for Alicia to marry a man from their church not some "hoodlum" with a mysterious past.

Alicia didn't care about her parents' opinion of the relationship. She loved him and wanted to be with him.

"What are your intentions with my daughter? Alicia is my pride and joy, my princess. She's the youngest of all my children. Do you think I'm going to let any man come in here and carry her away? She must not have described the kind of man I am."

"You daughter speaks very highly of you, sir. And to clarify my intention—my intentions are to marry your daughter one day. I love her more than any of those doctors or lawyers you'd set her up with."

"Marriage is not a game. Mrs. Riche and I have stayed married for over 20 years because we have a strong foundation. Alicia deserves a good man. Don't you agree?"

"Yes, I agree. I believe I am that man."

"For your sake, I hope you prove me wrong."

Dad's polite demeanor scored him a few points with Mr. Riche.

"Where are you from, boy?"

"Born in Philly, raised primarily in Japan."

"You're a nice boy. There are millions of girls who would be lucky to have you. You're just the wrong guy for my baby girl."

The Riches had not been on speaking terms with their daughter for about a month following the dinner. Alicia's separation from her close-knit family affected her emotional state. She called out of work for a doctor's appointment after missing her "monthly visitor."

Alicia called Dad after receiving the results.

"Babe, it wasn't stress. I'm pregnant."

"......."

"Are you there? Did you hear me?"

"This is so unexpected. I have a knot in the pit of my stomach."

"I'm freaking out, my parents are going to kill me. I can't go back to school or church. We have to get married ASAP. I can't have a baby out of wedlock."

"Your parents are the least of my concerns. The Black Hand will kill us for this. I didn't even start working missions for them, yet."

"We can elope... fly to Vegas. They won't know for a while. Then, we can run away, together. Your dad left you that money, we can move to an unknown island."

Circumstances did not permit the dream wedding every little girl fantasizes about. Alicia couldn't invite her best friends or have the perfect dress. She envisioned her father walking her down the aisle since she was 6 years old. Instead, Maurice disowned Alicia, leaving her to invest her time and energy into her future family. The "us against the world" mentality fueled their willingness to get married.

"I think we may be rushing into this marriage."

"You're telling me this on the plane to Vegas. We could've backed out of this wedding when we were at the airport."

"I think you're only marrying me because I'm pregnant."

"I love you and I love our future baby. My baby is going to have everything I didn't. A loving mom, a dad and a stable environment."

A taxi driver pointed out the famous Vegas attractions. The lights over-stimulated a guy who'd lived in the mountains for a year.

On the strip, Dad and Alicia found a 24-hour wedding chapel. They said their vows in front of an Elvis impersonator and made it official. Their wedding photo was taken in front of a spouting fountain with a disposable camera. The newlyweds rode a taxi to their hotel following a celebration at an exclusive nightclub.

"Hey babe, can you get some ice for the champagne?"

"Sure. I'll be right back. Don't move a muscle."

Dad whistled a melodic tune as walked to the ice machine. He bumped into Ivan the Terrible as he turned the corner. Dad dropped the bucket in dismay. Ivan handed him a first class plane ticket and a passport.

"I have a mission for you, ACE."

"I'm…um...busy."

"On your honeymoon, right? You knew the rules and chose to break them. Things didn't have to be this way."

"Please, give me one more night. It's my honeymoon, my wife will be crushed if I leave without at least saying goodbye."

"I don't make concessions for those who are stupid enough to break our rules. Let's go or maybe you haven't been properly incentivized."

Alicia flicked back and forth between the late night shows. Her new husband had not returned to the honeymoon suite. She called down to the front desk; none of the clerks had seen him. "No one fitting the description has come through the lobby. The hotel staff will keep an eye out for you, ma'am."

They played with fire and got burned badly. The joy my parents shared was instantly extinguished. There were other mercenaries available but the syndicate was not impressed with their other options. Victor was cognizant of Dad's martial arts training and a smart businessman always collects on his investments.

CHAPTER 12

SEVERANCE

Mom had to cobble together an excuse as to why Dad ran out on her. She told friends and family that he couldn't handle living in America anymore and moved back to Japan. My other grandfather, Mr. Riche smugly said "I told you so" after his daughter's personal business circulated the community. In the interest of their safety, Mom begged her family to stay out of the situation. No one understood why she was rejecting her own flesh and blood.

The first few months of Mom's pregnancy were tumultuous ones by any standard. After the Vegas fiasco, she returned to work and pretended as if nothing happened. Mom flew under the radar until the afternoon she was called into the boss' office.

"Come right in and close the door behind you. You're probably wondering why I asked you to leave the floor."

"Yeah, I have my show to get ready for and they haven't done my makeup and hair yet."

"That's what I wanted to talk to you about. No one is paying to see a pregnant lounge singer. Your ever-growing belly is losing me customers. I'm sorry but I am going to have to let you go."

"Don't do this to me, Mr. Rinaldi. I've been very loyal to this company over the years. I followed my heart and made a mistake. Who hasn't?"

"You know I do not tolerate any hints of disloyalty from my employees. The best option is to keep your mouth shut and pray nothing worse happens to you. Security, please escort this woman out of the building."

Mom plopped down on the bathroom floor with her arms wrapped around her knees. She rocked back and forth, fighting the urge to stare at the bottle of aspirin resting on the counter. With a flick of the wrist her pain could have ended. Mom contemplated ending two lives at once. How could she bring a baby into the same world where the Black Hand grows more powerful by the day?

As soon as her hand touched the bottle, the phone rang. Mom ignored the rings at first. She ignored them for as long as humanly possible. The ringing did not cease which baited her to pick up the phone. It was Sister Anita from the church calling to invite her back to the choir.

"Hey, girl. How you been?"

"Hi, Sister. I'm fine. You know I'm not one to complain. I've just been going through a lot trials and tribulations lately."

"The choir has not been the same without your angelic voice. You just disappeared one day—out of the blue. What's up with that?"

"Yeah...I--"

"--Pregnant."

"You kept my secret?"

"Well, I have been around for a long time, dear. Is that the reason you've been staying away from the church?

"You know how church folk are. I didn't want to be the center of Sunday morning gossip. The last thing I needed in my life was more judgment."

"Let people say what they want. Only God can judge us."

"You're right...but it doesn't mean it hurts any less."

Mom believed it was a message from God telling her not to give up. Surprisingly, she found support from the people she expected to judge her the harshest. Mom returned the bottle to its rightful place in the medicine cabinet and never considered suicide again. Truthfully, I was not very fond of Sister Anita as a child. Who knew she was responsible for not only saving my mother's life but mine as well?

Singing in the choir cleared her mind of the madness and lifted her spirits. The next Sunday, mom delivered an inspired rendition of *His Eye is On the Sparrow*. There was not a dry eye in the sanctuary after that amazing performance. The emotional outpouring stunned the congregation at the Baptist church. Reverend Johnson paused the service to thank Mom for baring her soul in front of everyone.

In the coming months, the ladies from the church helped out in various ways. They threw Mom a baby shower and even drove her to her doctor's appointments. Mom taught in the city literally to the day she gave birth. On the day I was born, Sister Anita was in the hospital room praying for no complications.

Dad made it to the hospital minutes before she was taken into the delivery room. He received a chilly response from the protective pack of ladies.

"What are you doing here?" Mom asked.

"What do you mean—what am I doing here? I was never going to miss the birth of my son," Dad replied.

"Tell me you cleared this with your bosses. I'm done making enemies out of those guys."

"Yeah, of course. I fought hard to get this time off. Trust me, it wasn't easy. They're still mad at me for what we did in Vegas."

Fifteen hours of labor culminated in the birth of a precious baby boy. The hardships of the previous nine months melted away once Mom held me in her arms. My parents' eyes met, both unable to address what had been left unsaid. There was no closure to the relationship. An outside force ripped them apart.

"Can I hold him? It's kills me to know that I will end up being a worse father than my own."

"Sure you can? Be careful with his head."

"Are we still naming him Phillip?"

"He's still your son, that hasn't changed. It's even more fitting that he has your name considering what we have going on."

The Black Hand only allowed father to have a couple of hours with his family. Any more time and it would've been impossible to tear him away. They used us as a tool to keep him under their thumb. From then on, our contact was few and far between, minimal at best.

The project ATLAS officials fabricated a thinly veiled cover identity based on Dad's real life. They gave him an internship position at a movie production company to learn the trade. The production company had been a foreign subsidiary of an American film corporation. The studio offered access to drug addicted celebrities, the best facial prosthetics and clearance to travel to remote locations.

The Black Hand staged the sale of the fledgling movie company. Dad invested the money Grandpa left him to buy the controlling stock in the company. He employed a well-known entertainment lawyer to draw up the contracts. Dad poured the rest of his funds into purchasing the latest in state-of-the art equipment and building sets. To keep costs low, everything had to be done in-house in the beginning. Dad developed the intellectual properties and wrote the screenplays. Kenzan hired the actors and choreographed the fight sequences.

The Baxter Production Company was formed and the hits did not lag far behind. Their movies struck a chord with movie audiences around the world. The low budget films banked more than quadruple the production costs and advertising budgets. Its unforeseen success complicated the plans of the Black Hand. Once someone becomes a public figure, his life is exposed to intense public scrutiny. They hired a new public relations team to manage the company image. Dad's cover made him out to be a new age socially conscious recluse and Kenzan was promoted as the hardworking face of the company.

The mercenary work and the movie productions formed a symbiotic relationship. Dad completed daring missions, which he used as creative inspiration for movies. (They obviously tweaked the storylines to hide the source material.) The action in his movies felt spontaneous, grounded and exhilarating. The plots fused the best of espionage and political thrillers. Dad believed the best stories are the ones based on reality.

CHAPTER 13

REINCARNATION

Dad had been experiencing memory lapses and bouts of amnesia for over a year. He sought insight from his former teacher and father figure. He returned to Japan after a taking a leave of absence from Project ATLAS operations. The Kaito family welcomed him with open arms and tearful elation.

"We are overjoyed to have you back with us. Takara and I missed you dearly. We did not believe you would ever come home."

"Sensei, I wish I was here under better circumstances. Since I lost my wife and son my mind has been unstable. My thoughts are unfocused and it has affected my work for the Black Hand."

"As you know I worked with your father for many years. I did things that went against my personal beliefs on life. For a long time, I refused to sell my soul to those devils. So they killed my brother to force my allegiance."

"Accept me as your student, again. Teach me how to survive in this world as you have done in the past."

"You are no longer a student of mine. Those days are over. There are no more lessons for me to teach you. The only man with the knowledge you seek is living at a monastery."

"Can you take me there?"

"Get some rest. We leave at dawn."

Ichiro began the next day when it was still dark outside. In the wee hours of the morning, he drove two hours and stopped outside the city of Kyoto.

"Go on, ahead. You have to finish this journey on your own."

"I don't think I'm ready," Dad replied.

"You are stronger than you give yourself credit for. Now go!" Ichiro commanded.

Dad opened the door, took a number of steps, and turned back. He mouthed the words "Thank you." Ichiro remembered how the same training changed his life. He was tested physically, mentally, and spiritually. To be able to provide that for someone else, not of his same blood, wouldn't have occurred to him in the past.

The summer heat made getting to the temple an arduous undertaking. Dad walked for miles, his shirt clung to his body. He asked a merchant for the directions to the temple. The merchant pointed him in the right direction. The ancient temple was off in the distance, situated within a mountain.

Dad reached a colossal gate at the entranceway of the monastery. It connected to a miles-long stone pathway, framed by magnificent sculptures. The trek ended when he stumbled upon a pair of buildings.

Upon entry of the first temple, there were disciples gathered for the Sunday ceremony. This temple had been chosen because of its welcoming stance to outsiders. A monk led a collection of devoted disciples in meditation. Following the ceremony, Dad approached the monk and asked for a moment of his time. The monk allowed him to speak.

"I am looking to be trained by the Roshi, Master Genko."

"The temple is full, the master will not train you." Tai Xi, the Senior Monk replied.

"I can't go back home without learning at the feet of the master. I've outgrown my old life."

Monks usually refuse a disciple's initial plea for admittance. It humbles the disciple; pride is left at the front gate. Tai Xi left him with no alternatives but to leave. Dad had nowhere to go and therefore bound to sleep in front of the monastery. When night came, the Senior Monk invited Dad to inhabit the lodging room for meditation.

On the fourth day, Tai Xi allowed Dad to come inside for the initiation ceremony. "You may sleep here for the remainder of your stay. This is also a place where you can meditate." Dad moved from the lodging room to one of the meditation hall. The brotherhood prepared him in fresh robes in anticipation of his meeting the master.

With great trepidation he met the legendary Master Genko for an interview. Master Genko was an older bald man, dressed in a black silk robe. The interview covered a wide spectrum of topics, ranging from simple to introspective.

"What is your name?"

"My name is Phillip Baxter II."

"Why are you here?"

"I don't know."

"Why are you here?" Master Genko asked, again.

"I am here for enlightenment. My sensei, Ichiro says I'm wandering in the sea of life."

"I see the same quiet resilience I saw in the eyes of my student Ichiro. The answers you seek have always been there, you are lacking awareness. We believe that everyone is capable of achieving enlightenment."

Master Genko respected the honesty of the young man who stood before him. He trained Ichiro when he was a young man, comparatively directionless.

Under Master Genko's rigid tutelage, trainees spend limitless hours in deep meditation. The monks possessed clarity of mind and heightened concentration. In the mornings, they tackled philosophical riddles.

Master Genko asked, "How does one know his purpose?"

"Gaining awareness leads to finding purpose," Dad replied.

"How does one gain awareness?"

"Human beings are already enlightened. We tap into that part of ourselves by using meditation."

Master Genko painted a black open circle onto a white canvas. "This circle is simple, yet profound, empty and full. The opening leaves room for enlightenment to flow inside of it continuously. Nothing and no one is perfect. We are perfectly imperfect beings. There is no single or correct path."

Dad gained a lifetime's worth of enlightenment in an incredibly short period. Mediation is real commitment and the monks didn't skip a minute of it. They meditated the same way, rain or shine every single day.

During his seventh month at the monastery, Dad was invited to participate in what is known as the O-bon Festival. Zen monks perform a ritual where they reach out to the spirits that have not reached nirvana. As humans these spirits were greedy, selfish and jealous. These spirits are cursed to stay in limbo, feasting on the corpses of the dead. To ease the suffering, the monks offer the spirits food.

On the third day of the festival, a vengeful Hungry Spirit possessed my father. His body convulsed as his consciousness was transported to an otherworldly plane. Minutes later, Dad's body stopped convulsing. He opened his eyes and found himself on the mountains behind the monastery. Something had changed; his demeanor and even the inflection of voice were altered.

The brotherhood noticed the subtle metamorphosis. Tai Xi griped to Master Genko for opening the doors to an outsider while denying the disciples of the city. A segment of the brotherhood agreed with those sentiments. "Master Genko has lost his mind in his old age. A new master must step forward."

A ringing gong signaled the start of the final day of training. As usual, Dad chopped logs to bring back to the monastery as part of his daily chores. Upon return, there was total silence, no movements or activity. He saw what appeared to be a hand poking through the bottom of a doorframe. Dads advanced towards the door and to his amazement, Master Genko and the rest of the brotherhood were dead.

Who could have committed this heinous murder? By his count, all the monks had been killed, except for Tai Xi. Where was the Senior Monk? There was no sign of him in any of the temples or on the grounds. Dad encountered Tai Xi in the meditation hall near the front entrance.

"Why did you do this to your brothers, Tai Xi? They did nothing to deserve your wrath."

"Follow me and your questions will be answered," Tai Xi replied.

Dad followed him into one of the compact backrooms. There was barely enough space for two people to comfortably fit. Tai Xi asked Dad to sit and wait for him. He returned with a mallet, chisel and a block of wood. Tai Xi used the tools to shape the wood by defining a nose and carving the eyes. He applied a liquid made from oyster shells to reveal the dents and scrapes on the surface, then smoothened out the mask. Tai Xi repeated the process over sixty times to clear away imperfections.

The monk presented the mask after hours of craftsmanship.

"I can infuse you with centuries-old wisdom and

unfathomable physical enhancements. This handcrafted mask is a conduit, which funnels the energies from the spirit world. All you have to do is place the mask over your face and your training will be complete."

"What makes you believe I want this great power?"

"All great men have a thirst for power, that is why."

Dad lifted the mask and held it squarely in front of his face. He held it up there for about thirty seconds but he didn't feel anything. He'd never performed the ritual so he wasn't sure he had done it correctly. Suddenly, he felt a rush of energy coursing through his veins.

The spirit granted my dad the ability to exceed what is considered the upper limits of human potential. Dad achieved the highest level of consciousness, a state called Samadhi. It's a state of perpetual meditation, the intersection of awakening and dreaming.

The Hungry Spirit released Tai Xi from its control.

"What has happened here? What have I done?" Tai Xi asked in disbelief.

"You killed the brotherhood of this temple. It's not a mystery why the spirit chose you over the others. He needed the seed of hate you carried, the hate that consumed you. It allowed the spirit to influence your actions. Now you have to live with this eternal shame."

"I grew tired of outsiders reaping the rewards of

our ancestors. I pleaded with the master to close the doors and he scolded me." Dad removed a Seppuku blade from his belt and held it out. "I have dishonored not only myself but this temple and all that it stood for."

Dad walked away from the temple without turning back. He paused when he heard the blade slicing through flesh and muscle.

Tai Xi sparked a flame that destroyed the temple. Hundreds of centuries-old artifacts were charred by the blaze. Dad was able to leave the temple physically unharmed but his mind continued to deteriorate. He wandered to a train station and rode home to Tokyo.

CHAPTER 14

HIT MEN VS HITAMEN

Project ATLAS hired father to eliminate Christopher Idemas, a successful mogul and philanthropist. Christopher was a former associate of the Yakuza crime organization who, a few years earlier, got into a heated dispute over the gang's cut of his profits. He quit the gang, moved to America and transitioned into legitimate business ventures.

Victor loathed the Yakuza and its affiliates. The modern Yakuza's image and leadership structure is based on the Italian Mafia's. They adopted the suit and tie style and even operated illegal underground casinos. The Japanese love to gamble and the increasing number of Yakuza casinos weakened business. Victor did not view imitation as a sincere form of flattery, especially when it affected his bottom line.

Christopher's financial advisor initiated a hostile takeover of the Tokyo High Rollers Casino. One of the Reginas reported the information to her boss who wasn't pleased. Victor declined the acquisition offer presented by the team of consultants. Nonetheless, Christopher pursued the merger, buying more and more stock in the company to backdoor his way in.

The rising tension between the Black Hand and the Yakuza had reached its boiling point. The rivalry escalated because casinos weren't the only rackets they competed in. The Yakuza had an extensive drug and human trafficking operation in conjunction of the gambling network.

Every year, Christopher held a prestigious masquerade ball at the New York Idemas Hotel. The proceeds of the event went to a charity of his choice. The crème de la crème in their respective fields made appearances. The security was extremely tight and the paparazzi came out in full force. Luckily, my father received a coveted invitation to the event, negating the need to infiltrate it.

Dad preferred killing targets in the course of their day-to-day activities. A home is an added physical barrier to overcome. Wealthy people live behind tall gates and hire private security. A homeowner knows the "ins and outs" of their home better than a stranger. It takes a considerable amount of time, effort and planning to effectively kill someone within the walls of their own mansion. Although killing people outside of their homes comes with its own share of difficulties, my dad believed that his strategic mind gave him a distinct advantage in neutral surroundings.

The masquerade ball was scheduled to commence in a half hour. With not much time left to prepare, Dad chose a gold, half-face leather mask to match his costume. He stared at his own reflection in the mirror, rehearsing the lines and mannerisms he intended to use for his cover. Dad altered his posture, facial expressions, and even the poses he intended on using for the red carpet.

Dad waited at the elevator for at least fifteen minutes. It finally stopped on the seventh floor and he crammed into it. Everyone must have been coming down to the lobby for the event.

As he entered the ballroom, Dad was immersed in an ultra-rich opulent lifestyle. The theme of the evening was 18th Century Europe. Everyone dressed in elaborate costumes and fancy masks. The tables were covered in fine linen tablecloths, expensive champagne and floral centerpieces. Dad socialized with young socialites, celebrities and oil tycoons. The talk of trust funds and Swiss bank accounts left him truly disinterested. Dad threw in a fictitious anecdote about wanting to renovate his second home in Martha's Vineyard. By the fourth glass of wine, he felt confident that he was selling the character.

Dad concluded the chitchat part of the evening and abruptly left the table. He excused himself to the restroom to analyze the layout. From the entrance he noted the two urinals to the left followed by two stalls. Adjacent to the stalls was a sink and toward the back wall was a window. Dad returned to his seat. The presentation was set to begin and he did not want to invite any unwarranted attention.

A strumming string quartet signaled the imminent arrival of Mr. and Mrs. Idemas. Christopher was a short unattractive Chinese man who married a retired American supermodel. The striking contrast in physical appearance couldn't be ignored though it had been mitigated by his handsome bank account and charming personality. Christopher and his wife, Paige, made their entrance amid flashing lights and mumbling. The photographers buzzed about Paige's gown and how great she looked in it.

Christopher shook wealthy hands on his walk up to the podium. His rousing opening joke about the forty thousand dollar plates "broke the ice." Christopher wholeheartedly applauded everyone for attending his annual charity event. He commented on the great cause that his foundation promoted. Christopher's foundation pledged to donate a large contribution for the advancement of breast cancer research.

Afterwards, played a heartwarming video chronicling the lives of women who suffered from the disease. A breast cancer survivor was asked to stand up. She tearfully thanked everyone for his or her laudable donations to help find a cure.

The guests congregated in the ballroom once the meal had settled. Christopher escorted Paige to the dance floor. Dad needed to get within arm's reach of the couple. He asked the young socialite for a dance. The woman had been making blatant advances throughout the night. They danced to one song and Dad moved within a foot of Christopher and his wife.

"Can I cut in?"

"Sure you can," Paige replied.

They switched partners and resumed dancing.

"A mask should never hide such beauty," Dad said.

"You're a real charmer for sure Mr...."

"Remember—no revealing identities before the unmasking hour, Mrs. Idemas. Let's switch the subject, shall we? So, have you been enjoying yourself so far?"

"I've been enjoying myself quite a bit, it's a wonderful cause we're raising money for. My best friend was diagnosed with cancer 3 years ago. I promised her I would help to find a cure. I'm hoping we can raise awareness and a lot of money for research," she said.

"My father died of cancer a few years ago so I get

how much this means to you. I commend you and your husband for taking such an interest."

It must have been hard not to get emotionally invested. Dad looked into her eyes knowing that he was on the verge of killing her husband.

"Do I make you nervous? You're sweating profusely," Paige said.

"I'm not used to dancing with famous supermodels. Please excuse my sweaty hands."

Christopher returned to his seat just as Dad had intended. At the end of the dance, Dad picked up a glass of champagne. He approached Christopher's table and clumsily spilled his drink all over him.

Christopher jumped out of his seat.

"I'm so sorry. I'm such a klutz sometimes. I'm going to clean this up," Dad said.

"It's okay, accidents happen," Christopher replied.

"Maybe you should go to the bathroom and use the mirror," another guest suggested. Christopher padded his suit as he scuttled off to the bathroom. Dad wiped off the seat for an extra minute to make it seem legit. He slipped a knife into his right pocket when no one was watching.

Dad followed Christopher's path to the men's bathroom. He pressed his ear against the door and heard the sink running. Dad made his way inside and saw Christopher wiping the jacket with his back facing the entrance. Dad crept up from behind and suffocated him with piano wire.

He dragged Christopher's body headfirst into the closest stall. Out of nowhere, a masculine voice grew louder and louder outside the door. Dad closed the door to the stall and ran into the other one. He hopped on top of the toilet seat and extended his arms to secure a balance.

A hit man entered the bathroom and walked right over to the first stall. His body cast a large shadow on the ground, pinpointing his position. The hit man stood there, peeking through the space of the door and its hinges. He identified Christopher's fresh corpse slumped over the toilet seat. "Someone got to him first, there goes our payday," he said. The hit man hastily walked towards the exit and stopped. He doubled back; he must have noticed that he hadn't checked the other stall.

The hit man stopped in front of the second stall and pushed the door in. Dad kicked it, sending him flying backwards towards the sink. Dad lunged. The hit man dodged the attack, throwing him off balance. Then he applied a sleepy hold, cutting off the oxygen. Dad fought but couldn't get out; the hit man had too much leverage. Time was not on his side, he almost passed out. Dad used his leg strength to drive the mercenary into the edge of the counter to break the hold.

Both men were down on the ground, gasping for air. The hit man wrapped both hands around Dad's neck and choked him. Dad desperately fought the adversary and gouged his eyes. The hit man screamed from the excruciating pain. Dad reached into his pocket and stabbed him in the chest with the butter knife. The man collapsed. Dad ripped off his mask but could not identify the gentleman. He unbuttoned his shirt as he searched for I.D. and discovered a Yakuza body tattoo.

The hit man was an elite member of a Yakuza kill squad. Coincidentally, he must have infiltrated the charity dinner as a guest as well.

The loud music drowned out the sound of the scuffle in the bathroom. Dad dragged the man into the stall with Christopher's body. A deep red trail of blood gushed out, staining the bathroom floor. Dad scrubbed the area with soap and paper towels. He flushed the towels down the toilet clogging it.

Unbeknownst to him, a pair of Yakuza mercenaries had been standing guard outside the door. They kept everyone else from entering the bathroom. Dad ruled out making a clean getaway. He opened the door and sprinted right by the two men. When they noticed he wasn't their partner, they triggered an EMP device that had been planted in the bathroom. The pulse emitted from the device shut off the power to the first two floors of the hotel.

The room was pitch black, the guests panicked. Crowds of people scrambled in the direction of the exits. The pushing and shoving produced a high volume of trampling victims. Dad could feel his personal space being invaded by multiple fast approaching figures. The mercenaries equipped with night vision goggles swarmed him. They attacked first. Dad valiantly fought back. It surprised the mercs how well he held his own against the highly skilled combatants. He blocked a number of kicks and punches. Eventually the sadistic mercenaries got the upper hand.

Police lights from outside penetrated the once unlit ballroom.

The leader of the Yakuza mercenaries propped him up by his arms. They landed series of hooks, rendering him nearly incapacitated.

"Let's get out of here, he already cost us the job. We can take credit for his kill anyway."

"He's right, the cops will be here any minute now."

The mercenaries fled the scene. Dad skipped out just as the police arrived.

The choice to leave the calling card saved my father's career. That card proved that ACE killed Christopher and not the Yakuza mercenaries.

ACE cornered the market on assassinations and the other hit squads grew frustrated. They weren't up to par with the newly established standard. It required a team to execute the types of missions ACE completed singlehandedly. They plotted his death, knowing it wouldn't come easily.

After the Idemas mission, Dad obsessed over it ceaselessly. When he got home he turned on the television. A local news outlet interviewed Paige about the unfortunate details surrounding her late husband's death. Paige cursed whoever killed the kind-hearted soul. She stated how difficult it had been to cope with the loss. They had three children together and the youngest recently entered school. Paige arranged the funeral service for the upcoming Saturday.

The board of directors was forced to suspend the acquisition of the casino for the foreseeable future.

Dad couldn't help but feel guilty. He found it much easier to deal with murder than to deal with the deception. As ACE he wore a mask, as Phillip he still wore a mask. His cover had effectively become his life. Project ATLAS purposely muddied the waters between the real and fake. He no longer owned his own identity. He hated the character he played at the charity dinner. The repercussions of his actions went far beyond whacking one man. He wrecked a charity event and may have harmed the development of future cancer research.

Who was Phillip Baxter II? I can't answer that question and sadly, I don't think he could either. When you're living a lie for so long, how can you know authenticity? What is real when each word is calculated and measured for a specific purpose or agenda? Dad questioned whether he had enough strength to live a murderous lifestyle. He could hide behind ACE for only so long before he faced the consequences of his actions. Dad became what he hated the most, a deceitful and untrustworthy person.

Grandpa had less of a problem with that. He welcomed the solace of being someone else for even a moment. Dad learned that everyone wears a mask at some point whether he or she admits it or not. It is not always a carved Japanese mask or a masquerade mask. It is an unseen untouchable mask, a schism and duality of self. That's why he selfishly bargained his family's happiness over his own integrity. It's easy to judge his actions. If you were in this predicament, would you do the same?

CHAPTER 15

PARANOIA

Alicia Baxter was undoubtedly the most influential person in my life. Out of necessity, she took on the roles of both "mommy" and "daddy." But she wasn't just a parent and caretaker. She was a strong, intelligent woman capable of almost anything.

As great as she was, there was one thing Mom couldn't do. She couldn't teach me how to be a man. That's not a knock on her; it's just the truth. As a teen, I rebelled against her strict rules and overprotectiveness. Mom smothered me and embarrassed us both in public. I even ran away once to exert my independence and caused her unimaginable pain. My actions were foolish in light of the fully justified anxiety she exhibited.

Mom was generally suspicious of everyone she came in contact with. The behavior I considered paranoid, eventually wore on me. She was so guarded that no man could chip away at the impenetrable wall that surrounded her heart.

From time to time, a situation arises that forces me to think back to those challenging moments in our relationship. Each lesson she taught me, every story I learned in Sunday School was for a specific purpose. It is as if she was preparing me for the day she wouldn't be around.

When I was eight years old, Sister Anita hooked Mom up on a date with one of her single nephews, Kyle. He was a young, eligible bachelor, and on paper he was a great match for her. He didn't even mind dating a divorced woman with a child. There wasn't a discernable reason why those two wouldn't hit it off.

Kyle seemed nice enough based on the first impressions. He was a gentleman who opened car doors and pulled out chairs. Kyle treated Mom well and showed her the respect she deserved. The guy had everything going for him except for one thing—he wasn't my father.

Mom constantly compared Kyle to the lost love of her life. I think even at eight I realized how unfair it was to him. That's when I stopped blaming myself for Dad's absence and started blaming her. I began lashing out and seeking out male guidance from the wrong crowd. My bad behavior snowballed, reaching a critical point at adolescence.

A controversial teacher's strike postponed my sophomore year of high school. Neighbor rallied against neighbor as the negotiations broke down between the teacher's union and the school board. Mom and I had an intense argument the morning of what should have been the first day of school.

I said, "You're paranoid about everything! All my friends get to have fun during the strike while I'm stuck at home with you. No wonder you're still alone. You're the reason I don't have a dad or even a stepdad." I apologized instantly though the damaged had already been done. My insensitive comments rendered her speechless; she could barely stand to look at me.

Mom sent me to my room after grounding me for a month. For twenty minutes, I laid in bed bouncing a tennis ball against my poster of Michael Jordan. I could not possibly get into any more trouble I thought. So, I decided to enjoy my last day of "freedom" with my friends at the mall.

An associate of the Black Hand paid our home a visit shortly after I had snuck out of the window. The shady gentleman aggressively pounded on the front door. Mom identified him as one of Victor's old friends known for making fatal house calls.

"I have an assignment for you, Ms. Baxter."

"I haven't worked for you or your boss in over 15 years. He fired me if I am remembering correctly."

"Why are you acting hostile towards me when I'm merely following orders? I'm here to give you an assignment that you are immensely qualified to perform. Our state's attorney general is setting his sights on the governorship. Getting credit for ending the teacher's strike would push him over the top. As a trusted teacher in this community, your endorsement of his proposals might sway the union. If Fredrick Coughlin gets elected with your help, it will go a long way in the eyes of the Black Hand."

"As long as you don't harm me or my son, we have a deal. I'm serious, no more scary guys at my front door."

When Mom opened the door to my bedroom. I wasn't there. I was off at the mall hitting on girls and causing mayhem. Mom assumed that I had been kidnapped by one of Victor's men. (It was a likely coercion tactic under those circumstances.) She called all of my friends' parents and drove around the neighborhood for hours. In dire straits, Mom called Dad's emergency phone number.

"Sorry to bother you, I didn't know who else to call."

"What's going on? Is something wrong with Phillip?"

"They got him. The Black Hand has our boy. You have to do something before it's too late!"

"First they abducted Kenzan's parents and now my son. This insanity has got to end. I'm heading over to the High Rollers' main office to demand answers. I don't care what anyone has to say about it." (The phone clicked)

I returned home at 10 o'clock and found Mom sobbing on the couch. Her eyes were red and the carpet was littered with crumpled tissues. It wasn't my intention to reduce her to tears. I didn't understand why she was so relieved to have me home safely. Mom squeezed me tighter than I'd ever been hugged. "Why would you scare me like that?" She said. "Mistakes have consequences and this one is no different. You haven't the slightest idea the trouble you've caused for your father." It meant nothing to me at the time but those ominous words stayed with me for a long time.

CHAPTER 16

HALLOWEEN MASSACRE

Matthew 12:33
"Either make the tree good and its fruit good, or make the tree bad and its fruit bad; for the tree is known by its fruit.
English Standard Version

In one day, I breezed through the handwritten journals Kenzan had entrusted to me. There's no defense for the emotional beating I sustained from that revelatory avalanche. I swallowed my pride and admitted to myself that I had misjudged my father's character. Clearly, he was not killed in a random carjacking. Somebody very powerful wanted him out of the picture. So few people had knowledge of his identity, I wondered if the Project ATLAS authorized his death.

The next time I saw Kenzan, we discussed the awful things I learned from the readings. Knowledge is power but sometimes it can be a curse. My grandfather had a hand in creating one of the world's most notorious terrorists. How do I accept that fact as part of my family's history? Essentially, everything I've been told throughout my life had been a lie. My mother's past, my father's past—all lies. She knew why he couldn't be with us the whole time. It does explain why she spoke so little of him.

"I'm done. I'm officially done with this whole ACE business. I tried to have an open mind and gave this an honest effort. The things I read are far worse than anything I prepared myself for. The crazy thing is my dad didn't want this either. Is this who I'm destined to become?"

"I believe it's your destiny to take up the mantle of ACE. The forces in the universe have already aligned to make this happen."

"I'm a regular guy and wish to stay as one. By picking up the ACE mantle, I'd be doing the complete opposite of that."

"You don't think the Black Hand is watching or listening to your every move? Fooling yourself into thinking this is a normal life does you no good. You are right in this regard. It is possible to break the cycle. I can train you. With my guidance you can destroy the Black Hand."

"If my dad couldn't do it, what makes you think I can? Maybe if I show them I'm not a threat they'll leave me alone. If I cause them trouble they'll eliminate me."

"Any Phillip Baxter is a threat in their eyes. They know you've learned their secrets and have probably ransacked your hotel room by now. Stay at your father's house where there's better security."

Kenzan understood where my objections originated. I was too busy lashing out to see the big picture. I focused on my options because my dad had none. He had no choice in succeeding Grandpa. I did have a choice and I chose to reject everything the ACE identity encompassed.

I moved into Dad's Yotsuya mansion, the same home where they held his funeral. I slept in one of the guest bedrooms during my first night there. I couldn't resist snooping through his stuff. I emptied the contents of his dresser drawers onto his bed and fished out a picture from my fifth grade graduation. On the back of the photo contained a note from my mom. Apparently my parents had more contact then I had been led to believe.

At that point, there were only two places in the house I had not seen, a room downstairs and the underground garage. The last room in the house was the only one to have the old-school sliding door. I slid the door open and scanned the area inside. It was a washitsu room, which means a traditional Japanese style room. It's a leisure room where hosts entertain their guests. This washitsu room served a different purpose. Dad redesigned it and anointed it his sanctuary of meditation.

Dad had a pair of exquisitely forged antique katana mounted onto the wall. I unsheathed one of the swords from the scabbard and examined the intricately engraved handle. The katana had a shinogi-zukuri style blade, a medium kassaki point and a prominent ridge crafted in the center. It must've cost a small fortune to collect these ancient weapons.

I dueled an imaginary foe in a shadow swordfight. Each slash cut the air, creating a mild gust of wind. Once I finished my Zorro act, I carefully returned the sword to its designated spot on the mantel.

In the corners of the room were wooden tansu chests containing various weapons most notably, the stainless steel hira shuriken. I touched the tips of the shuriken "Ouch!" I pierced my left index finger on the point.

Decorative hanging lamps illuminated the low meditation table. I kneeled in front of it and closed my eyes. I felt an unexplainable closeness to my dad, like his aura had reached out.

From there, I explored the underground garage Kenzan told me about. The driveway was the only access point to the subterranean levels. It worked as a car elevator that arose from under the asphalt surface. The elevator was operated by a state of the art computer system and powered by a hydraulic fueled cylinder mechanism.

All the vehicles had been implanted with a sensor, which detect incoming cars or motorcycles before hitting the ramp. The platform accommodates two cars and can carry up to 30,000 pounds. A tunnel connects the car lift to the underground garage. The garage is approximately 10,000 square feet and houses over 20 vehicles on its black and white graphite-tiled floor.

I gravitated to my father's black Kawasaki Ninja motorcycle. Coincidentally, I raced bikes in college even though I couldn't afford to own one. Nothing stopped me so I had no excuse but to take it out for a late night joyride.

I rode out to the industrial district in Chiba. I stopped at a traffic light in front of a tunnel and another biker rode up beside me. He gave me a nod, the light flashed green and it was on. Our rubber tires screeched and smoke arose behind our bikes. We zigged and zagged around slow moving sedans at dangerously high speeds. At 300 km/h the tunnel's lights created a warp speed effect on my helmet's visor. I checked my rearview, the biker had gotten smaller and smaller until he lost sight. I left him in the dust. Admittedly, I enjoyed at least one of the perks of my newfound wealth.

Later that night, a green blinking notification light awakened me. I reached over to the nightstand to turn on the lamp. Denise had sent a text message proposing we hang out since our previous encounter had been interrupted. I decided to face my demons and to take her up on her offer. What was her motive I asked myself? Was she going to apologize or spit out lame excuses? A part of me wished to see her in a bit of pain. Whatever pain she felt was a fraction of the pain she caused me. I had to keep it together and salvage what little pride I had left.

We met up at a local restaurant famous for its great seafood. Denise waited for me in the lobby. She looked amazing in her form-fitting jeans and blue top. Denise looked so good I momentarily forgot to be mad at her. They seated us at a table in the center of restaurant, our server cheerfully wrote down the orders. I ordered a salad as my appetizer and she ordered miso soup. I sat there twiddling my thumbs, waiting for our food to arrive. Denise smiled nervously and spent the next couple of minutes staring off into space.

"I guess I should start since I asked you to come here. First of all, I would like to thank you for agreeing to this. I know our relationship is complicated and you have many questions. I'm willing to answer those questions one by one."

"You lied, deceived and manipulated me. Do you realize how your actions have affected me? I'm going through a serious situation and now I have no one to confide in. There's nobody left for me to trust." I replied.

"I'm sorry. I don't know what else to say."

"It doesn't matter. I can't believe a word you say so what's the point? You've destroyed my ability to trust a single word anyone says."

"It's not so cut and dry. You're dad begged me to do it."

"That's no excuse. If he asked you to throw a bag of puppies over a bridge, would you do that too?"

What does that even mean?" Denise asked.

"I'm not sure. The point is that you have free will and exercised it."

"I owe him my life. Right or wrong I couldn't say,
"No."

Denise Leonard was born Denisse Leonardo in Luanda, Angola. She grew up knowing nothing but war. The continuous fighting had destroyed Angola's economy and infrastructure. Denise's father, Alberto, was a Portuguese man who owned a small diamond mining company. He was one of the rare owners who treated his workers fairly. Alberto married, Hasina, the daughter of his eldest Chokwe employee and provided a relatively comfortable life.

Denise's parents tried to shelter her from the harsh realties of life. They shielded her in the home, rarely allowing her to leave her block unsupervised. Denise's older brother, Iggi, was given more freedom because of age and gender. She protested the blatant double standard to deaf ears. In time, the Leonardo family learned that you don't have to go far from home to find trouble.

On September 29th, the nation of Angola held a presidential election. The party in power (the MPLA) prevailed in a contentious re-election campaign. Angola's opposition parties argued that the results were rigged. The

148

two main parties negotiated the terms of a run-off election since none of the parties received the required majority of votes.

In October of '92, Dad traveled to southeastern Angola to gain an understanding on spirit possession. He believed that if he could connect with his ancestors, they would help him to exorcise the spirit who plagued him. Dad tracked down a witchdoctor capable of performing the ritual at a dingy mystical shop.

Dad could only see the slender man through the crack of the door. The witchdoctor pressed his eye against the crack and stared back at him.

"How did you find me? Only a resourceful foreigner could've gotten this close."

"Are you the witchdoctor?"

"I prefer the title of prophet or diviner. Why are you here?" The witchdoctor eyeballed my father, up and down. "Is it a demon problem—you have? I specialize in demon exorcising. I can help you. Not for free though. You have to do something for me in return."

"Name it."

"Kill the priest who drove my kind out of the cities, Padre Jose Mendes. He feared the great power we possessed in our human form. Bring me his heart and his blood. A sacrifice is necessary to perform the ceremony anyway. Your hands must get much dirtier before they can get clean."

On October 30th, the army and police force

attacked the supporters of the opposition throughout the country. In three days, over 25,000 Angolans were killed for their loyalty to the UNITA. Dad arrived in Luanda on that day. He attended Sunday Mass two days later at the cathedral. Padre Mendes presided over mass in the midst of the Halloween Massacre. His parishioners prayed for a reprieve and an end to the bloodshed.

Padre Mendes blessed the Eucharist in preparation of the holy sacrament.

"And he took bread, gave thanks and broke it, and gave it to them, saying, "This is my body given for you; do this in remembrance of me. In the same way, after the supper he took the cup, saying, "This cup is the new covenant in my blood, which is poured out for--." A highly venomous golden-colored Cape Cobra struck the priest. It slithered off of the altar, expanded its hood and struck two more parishioners. "The devil has come for the Lord's people in His house!"

The parishioners cleared the cathedral. Dad scooped the cobra and confined it in a sack. Padre Mendes' breathing became shallow due to the neurotoxins poisoning his respiratory system. He lay there, in a paralytic state, unable to move. Padre Mendes watched as Dad unsheathed his katana, sliced open his chest and collected his heart. Dad's blood-soaked hands brushed over the priest's face to close his eyes. "Rest in Peace, Father."

Hours later, Denise's father heard a commotion out front. Alberto told the children to hide under the kitchen table. A group of mercenary rebels from the Republic of Congo had breeched the Leonardos' home. The MPLA hired them to take part in the military's power grab. The rebels took it upon themselves to demand a king's ransom worth of diamonds. (They often traded diamonds for the weapons required to continue their uprising.)

Alberto gave the rebels full access to his valuables. The apathetic rebels still killed both of her parents. Denise and Iggi shortened their breathing as they cowered under the kitchen table. Iggi placed his hand over his sister's mouth to ensure their silence. When the leader of the militia entered the kitchen, he saw four little feet quaking under the table. He lifted the tablecloth, pressed an automatic rifle to Denise's forehead and ordered the children to get up.

"Poor mulatto children it breaks my heart to do this to you. I also lost my mother as a child but this had to be done…she betrayed her people. The Portuguese are disgusting scum unfit to lace my boots. We only use them to promote our agenda." The leader snapped his fingers and pointed at Iggi. "I can mold you boy, in my image, the image of a real Simba. Take him and let's go. Leave the girl to fend for herself."

The leader kidnapped Iggi and vacated the premises. The remaining rebels looted the bedrooms. Out of the corner of her eye, Denise saw a man dressed in black clothing walking through her front door. He had on a white mask and hood covering his head. The man jumped over two flights of stairs in one motion. "A demon! God is punishing us for our sins!" The rebels shouted.

She immediately felt the rumble of multiple bodies hitting the floor above her head. The stranger came downstairs slightly tattered, carrying one of the rebels over his shoulder. He dropped the rebel on the ground and told him to send a message to his leader. "Fear the ninja!" Dad barked at the man.

Dad slowly turned to face Denise. He lowered the hood and removed the mask from his face. He crouched beside her and said these words to her.

"Look at my face, I'm not scary. The bad men are gone. Can I ask you a couple of questions, little girl?" She nodded her head. "Do you have any family to live with?" She shook her head twice. "I have a place for you to live. Do you want to live with me?" She nodded again.

Dad returned to the witchdoctor's shop with a shy new friend. Denise clung to him like celebrities cling to youth. He threw the witchdoctor the heart-filled container. Dad sent her out of the room so the adults could talk freely.

"The city has gone to hell in a day. I had to save the girl, she deserves a better life."

"You're a great and honorable man, far greater than me. I'm overjoyed the government continues to oppress its people. It serves them right for the treatment I had to endure." The witchdoctor picked out various symbolic items and stuffed them into a divination basket. "In an hour, I will take you to the water where the spirits gather. The river is a passageway into the spiritual world."

At the Kunene River, the witchdoctor donned a wooden tribal mask. He sang and danced in a circle to a rhythmic drumbeat. Dad asked him to expound upon the mask's role in the ritual.

"Your mask, it's really beautiful. What purpose does it serve in your ritual?"

"It's a Chihongo Mask. I wear it when I call upon the spirits for protection. My people also use them in performances."

"I have one of those."

"Do you?"

"Well, yeah. It's sort of the same. There is a great power contained within the mask."

"Bring it to me."

They sat at the edge of the water directly across from each other. The witchdoctor placed the Noh mask in the divination basket. He elaborated on the significance of each sacred object he had selected. The basket also contained two tortoise shells, a cat's eye, a dog's eye, the priest's heart and small figurines.

"The two tortoise shells represented a protective barrier. They allow me to see things, not of this world. The visions I am given are hidden from normal men. I receive visions of danger and death in people's futures." To stimulate the power of the shells, the witchdoctor sprinkled a special concoction on top of them.

One of the shells contained the cat's eye and the other contained the dog's eye. "A cat is a predator that hunts at night. Their eyes open wide and reflect brightly in the darkness. The eye connects me to the evil within the village." Conversely, the dog's eye guards his tribe against the spirit who exist on the outside.

The witchdoctor believed the spirit might've come from a foreign place. "I am an American but the spirit came to me when I was training at a temple in Kyoto. It possessed me during the festival of the dead."

The inclusion of a soldier figurine represented a fallen soldier or soldier who had died. "My dad was in the army, he fought in Vietnam. He's the reason I went to Japan and he's the reason I am here."

The Noh masked acted as an anchor tethering both men to the spiritual plane. The witchdoctor consumed the heart to empower him with the necessary strength to battle the evil spirits. Dad covered Denise's eyes, shielding her from the cannibalistic practice.

When darkness fell, Dad and the witchdoctor submerged themselves in the river. Denise nervously watched from sidelines. They emerged from the water as spiritual brothers forever linked by the event.

The witchdoctor gave Dad a small serpent charm as a gift.

"Keep this charm on you at all times. If you wear it, bullets and knives won't harm you." He also shared something shocking with my father as they parted ways. "You were never possessed, I am sure of it. Your mind has been playing tricks on you. Sometimes it is easier to believe you are possessed than to believe you have sinned."

"Oh my God. I did it…"

My father had a lesser-known form of dissociative identity disorder. His psyche had split into two distinctive personalities that often left him in amnesiac states. No one, not even my mother knew he lived with multiple personalities. The second personality did an excellent job of covering his tracks. He burned down the temple and distorted Dad's memories of the event.

"That's how I met Mr. Baxter, he saved my life," Denise said. "If he hadn't taken me, I would've been living in a shanty town amongst the orphans."

"I would've never guessed you lived through such tragedy. Whatever happened to your brother, Iggi?"

"I never saw him again. Mr. Baxter promised to help me find him if I protected you. He would've helped me regardless but I had an obligation to him." Denise's eyes watered, she put her hands over her face. "Excuse me." Denise got up from the table and went to the bathroom.

Not even a minute had passed before another woman had filled Denise's seat. It was very forward of her to approach a man at dinner with another woman. She looked awfully familiar and then I remembered from where. She was the woman from the boutique when I first arrived. The massive crowd kept me from getting inside the store and talking to her.

"I saw you from my section of the room and I had to talk to you. I noticed you the other day when I was shopping in the city. How rude of me, I forgot to say my name. My name is Marise."

"I'm Phil. I can't believe you remembered me."

"You don't exactly blend in here in Japan."

"Touché."

"Don't mean to rush but I have to return to my party. How about I give you my number?"

Marise grabbed my hand and turned my palm to face her. She pulled out a pen and wrote her number onto it. "Call me." She returned to her table the instant Denise exited the bathroom. As soon as she sat down Denise noticed the change in my expression.

"What'd I miss?"

"Nothing."

"Let's stay on topic. Do you have any more questions for me?"

"This may come off as sounding petty but I gotta ask you this question. Did my dad raise you as his daughter?"

"Mr. Baxter wasn't around much. Kenzan overtook the role of guardian in my life. Your dad did pitch in when he wasn't on assignments."

"Have you been back to Angola?"

"No, too painful. There's nothing there for me. Denise Leonardo died along with her parents. This conversation is depressing, it's time to change the subject."

Denise's eyebrows and nose scrunched together in unison. "Don't move. You have a red dot on your forehead." In a flash she flew over the table and knocked me to the ground. The man sitting behind me got sniped. His head rattled and fell into in the salad bowel.

Glass and debris filled air.

The customers scattered like ants.

"You saved my life."

"Don't thank me yet. We have to make it out of here alive. It appears the Black Hand is targeting you. That's definitely a warning shot. Stay low and head for the door." We crawled to my car avoiding bullets. We were safe inside of it; fortunately, it's armored.

"You should come home with me."

"Excuse me?"

"Not like that, Denise. Think practically, my house has the security of Fort Knox. An unknown shooter almost put a bullet into my dome. At least spend the night and in the morning we can sort things out."

"I'll spend the night because of something I hadn't told you."

"Surprise, surprise more secrets. Proceed."

"Late last night, I heard a loud crash downstairs. I rolled out of bed, walked halfway down the stairs when I witnessed a dark figure jetting out of the window. I searched the rest of the first floor for any other intruders. From what I gathered, the intruder only took a small trinket, your dad's serpent charm."

"Interesting…we've both been targeted within the last 24 hours. We should definitely consult Kenzan in the morning."

I parked my armored car at the edge of my driveway. We went inside and I escorted her to the guest bedroom. Unsurprisingly, Denise knew her way around the house better than I did. I lingered in the doorway of the bedroom, incapable of formulating speech.

"Do you have a shirt or something I can sleep in?" Denise asked.

"It's funny, you used to wear my shirts all the time…seriously awkward…I shouldn't have said that."

"You have absolutely nothing to apologize to me for. You had every right to feel taken advantage of. It's not fair what I've done to you. I'm the one who has to accept the blame for the mistakes I've made."

"You're being too hard on yourself. Yeah, you did a bad thing for the right reasons. You saved my life tonight and probably did countless times without my knowledge."

"You're a lot like him, you know. He was such a compassionate person. He let his actions speak for him on most occasions."

In the morning, I called Kenzan to fill him in on the events of our night. He rushed over to the house in a panic. The recent attacks strengthened his position on me becoming ACE. By claiming the identity as my own I could repurpose it. There hadn't been anyone who could challenge the mighty Black Hand. The general populace is too preoccupied to ask the proper questions and the rich benefit from the manipulation of political systems.

Kenzan and I strolled the garden of the estate for a

bit. He used this opening to make a final impassioned appeal. We paused in front of the cherry blossom trees and he picked up a petal from the weeping willow branches.

"Do you know the difference between you and your father?" A proper response escaped me. "The difference between you and your father is that he knew how to let go and accept the struggles of life."

I listened intently, my ears perched a millimeter higher on my head than usual. Kenzan continued, "Come, look at the beautiful petals of this cherry blossom tree. These petals exemplify the transient nature of life. The lifespan of this flower is only about a week before the petals wilt and fall to the ground. People from all over the world flock to the cherry blossoms because of its inherent beauty yet equally fleeting existence. The flower has become the embodiment of Japanese culture. It has also been tied to the concept known as mono no aware."

I interrupted Kenzan before he had finished describing the concept of mono no aware. "It's not adding up to me. So I'm supposed to be miserable for the rest of my life. That's what you consider honorable? My dad was so unhappy that his mind created multiple identities to deal with this craziness."

"If you let me finish I will explain it to you. Mono no aware is loosely translated as the sensitivity of things. It means being more sensitive towards living and nonliving things. The wilted petal is more deserving of appreciation than the living flower. There is beauty in sadness and character is developed through sorrow. The people of Japan are characterized for their stoicism even when facing death. This resolve was tested many times during the twentieth century, especially during World War II."

Kenzan plucked a ripe cherry from the tree. "Losing his family was extremely painful for your father. He was only able to let go of negativity because he accepted his burden. His miserable existence provided you safety and an assurance of a normal life. To your father that was an acceptable trade. In the same manner, the cherry blossom tree bears healthy fruit even if the flowers are wilting. That's not to say that your father never succumbed to despair. When he was overcome with sadness, he gazed upon the trees and they reminded him to be strong. Do you know why he also named you Phillip?"

"No, it hasn't been explained to me and it wasn't included in the journals."

"He named you Phillip because the first two never got it right. Your dad bet all of his chips on you. His death will ultimately be in vein if you fail because of immaturity."

"You've sold me on your idea. I trust you to lead me in the right direction. I'll accept the family legacy in an attempt to repair the damage ACE has inflicted on the world. Too many have suffered, too many have died at the hands of the wicked."

Because of the madness, my conversation with Marise had slipped my mind. I called her to set up a date. At 10:00 pm, she introduced me to one of the hottest spots in Tokyo. It's in the Great Gai area where the alleyways are really narrow. I was almost claustrophobic by the time we reached our destination.

Only regulars are allowed inside, Marise vouched

for me at the door. The bar played a good variety of American Pop and International Hip-Hop. Its atmosphere was electric, the crowd swelled with each passing minute it seemed. The DJ even gave me a shout-out from his booth, the whole crowd cheered. We went outside, away from the blaring bass to chat.

"You're very popular in Japan. Every time I'm around you, people lose their minds."

"It's not popular on account of anything I've accomplished. It's my dad's cloud that hangs over my head. He's the great one, not me. "

"Your greatness, my greatness doesn't rely on who our parents are. Stop doubting yourself. They created an image for him, it's all smoke and mirrors."

On our second date, Marise and I partied at an exclusive dance club. Sometime after midnight, a police taskforce raided the place. They were in search of illegal drugs and the dance environment is known for having them. Marise and I were taken into custody and released once the police heard my name. "You and your friend are free to go. My apologies for wasting your time."

Marise was such a mystery to me. She was self-assured and supremely down to earth. Marise had a glow about her, an exuberant spirit, which drew me in. She had a fashionably funky style that I hadn't seen before. She wore extra large framed glasses, floral-patterned outfits and definitely pulled off the nerdy chic look.

"I'm afraid of what you have planned for our third date. We're just lucky my name is golden in these parts."

"How was I supposed to know the police would raid the club? And who said I'll let you take me out again?"

"I said it."

"Your American arrogance rears its ugly head. It's a turnoff to most, not to me though."

The time-consuming training sessions with Denise and Kenzan conflicted with my personal life. I trained from morning to night in jujitsu, judo and capoeira. My lack of time bothered Marise. She loved the nightlife and encouraged me to get out more. She pushed me to live fast and to take more risks. I knew Kenzan would object to me staying out at all times of night so I kept my relationship a secret from everyone. Hypocritically, I fell into the same trappings as everyone else.

CHAPTER 17

ROGUE

I thought we could handle things on our own. We were a formidable bunch, heavily armed and proficient in multiple forms of martial arts. The recent attacks placed us firmly in uncharted territory. I weighed the pros and cons of involving the weird CIA agent. Kenzan thought it was a wise decision to make the call. As much as it pained me to admit it, he was right.

Agent Cole came right over and I spilled the beans on what had transpired since I arrived in Japan. He wasn't as alarmed as I expected him to be. Steely-eyed and expressionless, Agent Cole reacted like someone who had received confirmation rather than revelation.

"What's the deal, Cole? There's something you're not telling me. I've been straight with you and that wasn't easy."

"Okay, okay I'll level with you. I was getting info from an unofficial informant. Your dad was the man who was informing me on inner workings of the Black Hand. He couldn't escape but he did work to take them down from the inside."

"Why, you Cole, with the amount of available agents in the CIA? Tell me what makes you so special."

Adrian Cole was a young and idealistic agent stationed at Camp Chapman in Khost, Pakistan during the mid to late 2000s. As a counterterrorism operative he had been tasked with collecting human intelligence. Part of his job entailed forming and maintaining strong relationships with the people of this country. Cole, like everyone else was obsessed with neutralizing the threat of the Al Qaeda leadership.

The CIA turned detainees into double agents with hopes of dismantling them from within. An Afghani double agent, Kaleem Massoud provided the CIA with vital information on Al Qaeda. The CIA offered Kaleem a deal where he received a clean slate in exchange of his indispensable information. He took the deal out of fear and eventually became one of the CIA's most trusted informants. After a few months, they stopped checking him at the front gate, even though it's protocol. That gesture epitomized the lengths to which the government had been willing to go to acknowledge his trustworthiness.

Cole interacted with the Afghanis regularly and gained their respect in ways that none of the other operatives could duplicate. Something about Cole's personality captivated everyone he came into contact with. He didn't do too badly with the ladies either. The women on the base routinely got lost in the depths of his piercing blue eyes. The station chief asked Cole to work closely with the informant, taking advantage of his natural charisma. Kaleem's hostile vibe agitated most operatives and the CIA did not risk souring the relationship.

Rather than treating the Arabs as sources of information, Cole treated them like human beings. He learned about their families and even knew the names and birthdays of Kaleem's kids. Two of Cole's friends, Chip and Buddy warned him not to get to close, blurring the lines of professional and friendship. Cole denied it vehemently. He upheld the belief that his relationships would save countless lives.

Kaleem came in one afternoon with what he called a "huge bombshell", regarding the Taliban's movement in Pakistan. He met with Cole, the chief and a number of top agents.

"I'm raising my demands and I need it verified in writing."

"You're getting ahead of yourself, Mr. Massoud," the station chief replied.

"I've acquired the location to bin Laden's current whereabouts. I want the clean slate you promised, the reward money for his capture, and protective services until I exit Afghanistan."

"You drive a hard bargain Mr. Massoud. If your information checks out, you'll get everything you asked for and then some."

"I'm a reasonable man. I deserve fair compensation. The president's going to award you a medal and history will call you heroes. My demands are justified considering the dangerous position you've placed me in."

The president and his intelligence advisors grappled with their next move. Bin Laden had been on the move for years and the United States could not afford to play it safe.

"Mr. President, it's in the best interest of our nation to strike ASAP. Our satellites have established a bin Laden-looking individual, is at the safe house. We may never have this shot again. There isn't enough time for us to call in the Seals. However, there is a small paramilitary unit already in Pakistan capable of completing the mission."

"Make it happen."

Agent Cole led a secret kill squad affectionately nicknamed, the Sweepers. This squad was a collection of expert marksmen with type A personalities. Few were able to last in this elite fraternity tasked with cleaning up the dirtiest of Washington's messes.

All the squad members wore ballistic skull masks in the field. No one is quite sure where this tradition originated. Cole claims it started as a joke that quickly caught on. I heard from other sources that it was done to enhance their intimidation factor.

Under the president's order, the Sweeper Squad raided a fortified compound in Abbottabad, Pakistan. The unit stormed the house blanketed in darkness, donning night vision goggles and tactical gear. Half the men land on the roof from the Blackhawk helicopter. The other half blew the doors and charged through the rear entrance.

The Sweeper agents set their sights on the upstairs after clearing the downstairs. Agent Cole's unit busted the door open to the first bedroom. The Sweepers intruded on two spooked little girls crying in the corner of the room. "No Geronimo! I repeat, no Geronimo!" The agents rushed the second bedroom. "I got your six!" Cole shouted.

A man disguised as bin Laden sprang from the doorway and detonated an IED explosive. The shock waves catapulted Cole down a flight of stairs.

Agent Cole regained consciousness 4 hours later but something wasn't right. He couldn't hear anything except a high-pitched noise. The hearing returned intermittently, alleviating Cole's fear that one of his senses had deserted him. Dr. Morris pointed out that hearing loss is a normal injury resulting from close contact to explosions. She was confident that he'd make a full recovery and retain his hearing.

Cole had a litany of tertiary injuries, which included head trauma and a fractured arm. "Dr. Morris, I haven't been able to speak to Chip or Buddy. Can someone please wheel me to one of their rooms?"

"They haven't told you?" Dr. Morris said.

"Told me what? No. This can't be happening, they can't be dead. They're the toughest SOBs I've worked with." Cole replied.

"Frankly, it's a miracle that you're sitting in front of me. You're the only one who made it out of the safe house alive. Your tumble pushed you out of the immediate radius of the blast."

"I'm the only one who survived? Those guys had children and wives and…" Agent Cole's head throbbed in pain. "My head, it hurts."

"We have to run CT scans and MRIs, we suspect serious head trauma. Feel free to inform the nurses or doctors of any symptoms you're suffering from."

"Dr. Morris, I haven't been able to speak to Chip

or Buddy. Can someone please wheel me to one of their rooms?"

"Short-term memory loss —check."

Cole nearly suffered a nervous breakdown once the death of his colleagues sunk in. Why was he the only one whose life was spared? What purpose did his life serve? He replayed the memories of the attack over and over in his mind.

Agent Cole had never dealt with this kind of adversity. He had been a winner and overachiever for as long as he could remember. Agent Cole performed exceptionally well on the required CIA exams and had been quietly groomed for a position in Washington, D.C. someday.

The medical staff ran the full battery of tests to evaluate Agent Cole's mental and physical condition. The psychologists questioned his readiness to handle such a stressful position. He was only weeks removed from the traumatic event, which claimed the lives of his fellow agents. The reports factored in Agent Cole's memory loss issues as a major reason why he is no longer fit to serve.

CIA officials debriefed the only survivor of the botched tactical mission. The failure of the classified mission brought the activities of the secret squad to light. The officials promised Cole it wasn't an interrogation but that's not how it came across. His close relationship to Massoud cast a shadow of suspicion over him. An operative of his caliber does not hesitate to kill. Cole should have taken out the imposter with two shots before he set off the explosive.

Agent Cole recovered in a military hospital while the war on terror raged on outside. HIs station chief visited him to check on the progress and to provide encouragement. The chief also briefed Cole on the current mission parameters issued from Washington. The base attack heightened the United States' operations in the Middle East. They had detained close to 100 suspected terrorists indefinitely. Cole believed the detainees were being tortured in retaliation for the death of their colleagues.

"You guys aren't holding them because of what they know. You guys just want to punish them for what they've done to us." The chief didn't even try to fight him on the argument.

"This is the kind of war we're engaged in. The other side is bombing schools and local businesses. A trusted informant conned you and the people of our great nation. Someone has to pay. Examples are made. The terrorists have to know it's impossible to attack the United States without facing retribution. Don't worry yourself over this stuff, just focus on getting better. I'm expecting you back at the base when you're ready."

"To be frank, we're fighting a war perpetuated, sustained and based on lies. We've lost the moral high ground. It's a slippery slope."

The brush with death had a profound effect on Agent Cole. He had never acknowledged the inevitability of death. Everything was going as planned until something took that away from him. A person he trusted, a person who spoke of the injustices of this world became the one to facilitate the worst injustice of his life. Kaleem hated the hypocrisy of America and could not see the hypocrisy of Al Qaeda who has committed their fair share of atrocities. How do you differentiate the good guys from the bad guys when there are only varying shades of gray?

Cole couldn't do anything about it from his hospital bed, hooked up to wires. He dismissed every recommendation given by his doctors, frustrating them in the process. Cole asked for third and fourth opinions, looking for a positive one. He wasn't deemed fit to return to the field by any of the physicians, destroying everything he had worked towards.

The CIA sent Former Agent Cole home to rehabilitate closer to his family and friends. His mother wanted him to consider what his life would be like without the CIA. "You can still help the world from your home. You don't have to be in Afghanistan to be a hero, remember that."

A mother's words carry weight; it makes a man search deep within himself. There are different kinds of heroes, Cole evolved into a new kind. He created a blog where he gave detailed accounts into the waterboarding techniques employed by the U.S. government. At first, the blog was a small blip that got a few hits a day. Then a couple of thousands hits were recorded and the media eventually noticed. Shortly thereafter, government officials came to the house. Cole's honesty while admirable nearly landed him in prison. Fortunately, the lawyers negotiated a deal for no jail time. The only thing that saved him was the anticipated PR nightmare. An injured CIA agent jailed for releasing secret enhanced interrogation details would've turned him into a folk legend.

The intelligence community ridiculed Cole on their

message boards for either being a spy or brain damaged. He must have lost his mind after his accident they thought. Friends reached out to Cole to hear his side, he didn't respond.

One morning, Agent Cole pulled back the blinds only to find the paparazzi had been camped outside the window. Agent Cole denied every interview from the morning talk shows or major news networks. He was either praised as an unlikely hero of human or vilified by the collection of television pundits. They debated whether his motives were altruistic or opportunistic. They invented outlandish rationales for why he would "out" his own country.

Cole's house had no bars but it was no less a prison than any maximum-security facility. He struggled with the realization that the battle for truth is burdensome for those who choose to take arms. The CIA fired Cole as soon as a new hot story replaced his in the consciousness of the public. No surprise there, it was to be expected. That meant starting over without having advantage of his years of experience to rely on. A quick Internet search of his name removed him out of contention for many jobs.

Agent Cole's blog angered the inner circle of the Black Hand. They hired Dad to eliminate him swiftly and cleanly.

Four days had gone by after the ordered "hit" and Agent Cole had managed to slip the clutches of death. He opened his car door and sat in the driver's seat. Dad awaited him in the backseat. Cole placed the key in the ignition, then felt a sharp knife against his throat.

"Why did you reveal the torturous actions of your

government to the media? Do you have a vendetta against the CIA or something?" Cole had refused to disclose his reasons to anyone outside of his family. It wasn't based on tarnishing the reputation of his country or to receive accolades for exposing the CIA.

"I love my country, always have and always will. I regret nothing."

"Then you're the right man."

"The right man for what?"

"To take down the organization that controls the CIA and every other major institution. We're going to gut them from the inside-out."

"I believe in the merits of your mission, I believe in America's leadership role in the world. That's why I opposed the human rights violations to such a degree. The United States needs to regain its moral standing." Cole reminded Dad of another man who returned to America disillusioned with warfare. Giving him a purpose, not sympathy saved him from falling into depression.

This meeting occurred months prior to my father's death. Former Agent Cole partnered up with him to subvert the Black Hand. At the end of the meeting, Dad handed Cole a burner phone and told him to pack up his life and move to Japan. Dad and Cole had to keep a comfortable distance not to tip off the Black Hand to their alliance. Dad still performed their missions as ACE and ran the company. He made Cole promise to reach out to me if anything happened to him and to keep me safe when I learned of the conspiracy.

After months in Japan, they realized they hadn't collected any substantial evidence capable of incriminating members of the Black Hand. The Card System was designed to be discreet for this very reason. Cole wanted to discuss the other options on the table. "I do have something we can use," Dad said.

In 1996, Dad came into possession of a recoding that linked current and former members of the U.S. government to the death of JFK.

Project ATLAS authorized the assassination of former CIA director, William Colby. He's credited for exposing the biggest secrets of the CIA in the 55 Congressional hearings he testified in. The administration expected him to bury the truth about the clandestine services. Colby's refusal to tow the company line resulted in his unceremonious firing by President Ford in 1975. To say the Black Hand disliked this man is an understatement. His high-profile enemies laid in wait for over 20 years to exact their revenge.

On a Sunday in April, Colby ate dinner alone at his Cobb Island, Maryland home. His wife, Sally was visiting her mother in Houston. Dad casually opened the front door, pulled out the seat next to Colby and sat down.

"You left the front door unlocked. Not a smart move by a man in your position."

"What's the alternative? Living in fear—delaying the inevitable?"

"You knew in your heart this day was coming. You had to know the outcome when you rocked the boat. You may take this with a grain of salt but I respect you."

"I ran an organization obsessed with intelligence, lies and truth. You think I wouldn't be able to determine a lie if I heard one. I do believe you. That's why I'm handing you this tape."

"What's on this tape?"

"The answers to the biggest crime of our century. One day, when you have nothing left to lose…release it to the public."

The next day, a neighbor noticed Colby's disappearance and alerted the local police. Journalists swarmed Colby's small cottage home for days. The authorities found his decomposing body washed up on land almost a week and a half later. Dad staged the assassination to resemble a canoeing accident. According to the medical coroner's report, Colby had a heart attack and drowned. William Colby had no heart-related preexisting condition and only small traces of water in his lungs.

Dad converted the recording into an encrypted audio file and transferred the file onto a flash drive. He locked it somewhere for safe keeping until they amassed enough evidence to go forward with. He trusted Cole with the location of the flash drive just in case anything happened to him.

Dad had been unreachable for days; it wasn't like him to not return phone calls. Cole turned on the cable news and was floored by the segment on Dad's passing. By the time Cole got in touch with me, he had already known the truth.

"Why didn't you tell me this the first time you

talked to me".

"I'm not sure, I can't fully remember our first conversation. You're grieving the death of your father I probably wasn't sure you were ready to hear it."

"Where's the recording?"

"I forgot where I put it but I know it's "safe." I wrote a note to myself."

"We have to find the flash drive. The people who broke into Denise's house must've done so thinking it was there. Retrace your steps, do whatever you have to do to retrieve it. In the meantime, I'm going to prepare for the showdown with the Black Hand."

CHAPTER 18

BLUEPRINT

Two things had been made unmistakably clear for me: Firstly, I was in a uniquely qualified position to oppose the Black Hand. I knew the star players and owned a copy of their playbook. I devised a series of plans to cripple the Project ATLAS operations. I created the term "Counter-Assassin" to describe my new undertaking.

Secondly, if I really went through with this Counter-Assassin role, I'd instantly paint a bull's-eye on my back. Everyone, good guys and bad guys alike would view me as a menace. There's no way for law enforcement to differentiate my actions from those of the past ACEs and the Black Hand would despise me for spoiling their schemes. The more I thought about it, the more I reveled in the idea.

Denise and Cole squabbled over the route I should follow. Denise naturally favored my father's approach. She worked closely with him and saw the effectiveness of his methods, the methods employed by ninjas for hundreds of years. Cole's former life revolved around the CIA, he automatically assumed I'd follow in my grandfather's footsteps.

"Don't listen to this James Dean wannabe. Don't forget he got fired from his last job," Denise said.

"The CIA created and developed the concept of ACE. It's wise to have an understanding of the tactics they'll use against him," Cole responded.

"I'm really getting tired of your company. You strut around this house in your leather jackets and sunglasses at night. You've added nothing to our group except more problems. Phillip II trusted you and you fell short miserably."

The bickering had reached a personal level. I could no longer sit on the sidelines. "Come on guys, we're a team who has a monumental task to complete. It's up to us to save the world. The pressure is weighing on each and every one of us. It's not an either-or situation. I value what everyone brings to the table. Martin Luther King incorporated the teachings of Gandhi and look how that turned out. You're the closest thing I have to a family and I would appreciate it if we treated each other civilly."

The benefit of stepping into an established role is the fact that I didn't have to start from scratch. I only had to improve on the work of the earlier versions. I could pick and choose from what worked and discard other aspects. For example, my dad was known for his adaptability and my grandpa was known for his strategic intellect. How could I incorporate these traits into my interpretation of the ACE character? Both of the previous Phillip Baxters were soldiers of fortune of differing sorts. Their personality traits suited the types of lives they lived. One was an army pilot and the other, a spiritual warrior. What did I bring to the table? I'd been a history teacher raised in the household of an elementary school teacher. Not really an imposing identity when compared to that of my predecessors.

As a substitute teacher, I was used to implementing someone else's lesson plan. In our field, you sometimes have to hit the ground running on the first day. You enter unfamiliar environments, unsure of the customs and attempt to assert dominance. Challenges are met head-on; the first to blink forfeits their perceived power. My career as a substitute ended the day I claimed my inheritance.

Father and Grandfather had a weakness I don't share—they had families. The Black Hand controlled them with the threat of death or bodily harm to their loved ones. I had no weakness, no attachments and no family because of the Black Hand. They robbed me of a father and my mother, a husband. I had nothing worth living for, no one to call my own.

Attire & Gear

Since I didn't originally plan on staying in Japan, I ran out of clothes within weeks. Denise dragged me to the shopping district to purchase a whole new wardrobe. Somehow, I spent the entire afternoon trying on the types of clothing she believed fit me best. She upgraded my casual style and infused a touch of sophistication.

Black suits are the common business attire in Japan. If you expect to be taken seriously in Tokyo, you should have on a black suit, white shirts and a solid tie. Denise suggested I pick out the suits I'd wear as ACE. The other ACEs only wore suits when receiving missions. I would wear them out in the field. My tastes trended towards single breasted, two button modern style suits with high peak lapels. I bought a rack of skinny ties and leather driving gloves to complete the look.

Mask

My dad had a special connection to his Noh mask, a connection I could not duplicate. It acted as a connection to a spiritual world. I considered going with a ski or even a hockey mask. Cole surprised me with a mask of my own. He modified the Sweeper Squad skull mask his team wore in combat.

The bulletproof mask is comprised of a Kevlar and plastic composite. It covers from the top of the head, vertically and ear to ear, horizontally. An adjustable harness is attached to the sides, which secures the head in place. To incorporate the ace of spade's trademarks, a large letter "A" was painted on the forehead above the metal mesh eye shields and the nose bone was stylized to resemble a spade.

"There's a reason I'm passing on my mask to you. My time as a Sweeper is over…yours has just begun. You're in a position to clean up the messes created by the previous ACEs. The difference between us is that you're not a soldier. You have the autonomy to make the calls as you see fit. My squad had no conscious, no agendas; we were good soldiers fighting for something bigger than ourselves. Somewhere along the way I lost sight of what's important. This thing saved my life and granted me a second go 'round. It may do the same for you."

Headquarters

When I moved into Dad's house I was sure it would remain intact. I realized that wasn't feasible when the construction of ACE Headquarters got underway. I removed the weaponry and mercenary related gear out of the washitsu room. The room is meant for relaxing and fellowship. I returned it to its original purpose.

To prevent overcrowding in the garage, I donated 10 or so cars. I'm only one man and did not need that many cars. Why not give to the less fortunate? I filled the extra space with an armory, sword rack and a glass case where I showcased the Noh mask.

The house was in dire need of a technological upgrade. One of Cole's old CIA connects retrofitted the computer systems with illegal black market software. He updated our systems to include facial recognition technology, satellite fields and hacking programs. I now had access to government files from Moscow to Beijing and the coveted servers of the world's best intelligence agencies.

Weapons & Equipment

Cole instructed me on the cloak and dagger tradecrafts of the CIA. He showed me how to work effectively without having to engage physically. At the same time I improved my accuracy with firearms for the times when conflicts are unavoidable. "The Walther PPK handgun is lightweight and easily concealed. You should carry two 9mm Beretta pistols and the Walther PPK in your leg holster," Cole insisted.

Weapons & Equipment include:

- Grenades/Smoke Bombs
- Firearms
- Antique Japanese weapons
- Covert bulletproof vest
- Grappling Hooks
- Radio communication devices

- Spade-shaped shuriken
- Retractable blade Katana

CHAPTER 19

THE CANDIDATE

In late October, a startling news report signaled an escalation in the war against the syndicate. A series of classified intelligence documents leaked to the American public anonymously. The documents exposed the NSA's secret surveillance program known as PRISM. The U.S. government had been monitoring the Internet activity, emails and phone calls of American citizens. The administration dismissed the claims as "unfounded" and "bogus" accusations.

The secretary of state reiterated that under various acts and provisions, the government has authority to investigate suspected terrorists. "Upholding national security is our ultimate goal and surveillance is a must. Let's be clear, this is not an abuse or overreach of power. We are not monitoring law abiding citizens and we're not collecting the information for any ulterior motives."

The secretary of state's speech did nothing to quell the public outcry. Conversely, the coverage of the NSA leak opened a dialogue on the scope and reach of government. The Governor of Philadelphia, Fredrick Coughlin lobbied criticisms at the president for overstepping the boundaries of his office. "Our civil liberties are under seize, our privacy is now a figment of the past. We elect presidents, not tyrants in the United States of America. That's why I'm throwing my hat in the ring. I am officially running for the office of the President of the United States."

Days later, four terrorist attacks occurred on U.S. soil. Two governors and two senators were killed in targeted bombings. Governor Coughlin was assigned a temporary secret service detail while the FBI conducted its investigation. "Isn't it ironic," Governor Coughlin said during a radio interview. "The monitoring program is supposed to be keeping us safe. Ask your callers how safe they feel? When I'm president, Americans will not live in fear or in tyranny. There is a balance that doesn't have to compromise our ideals."

Governor Coughlin's campaign manager, Robert Donovan rounded up prospective donors for a fundraising event. "Governor, I'd love for you to meet one of your biggest campaign contributors. This is Victor Rinaldi of the High Rollers Casino franchise. He's prepared to sign a big fat check tonight." Coughlin shook Victor's clammy hand and brought him out onto the balcony.

"Governor, I've followed your career from the very beginning. I came to personally congratulate you on receiving the presidential nomination."

"We're more than a year out from the Iowa caucus. Your prediction is kind of premature."

"It's not a prediction, it's an eventuality. We've already decided that you're going to win the nomination."

"And who's "we?""

"We are an organization who has a stake in your ascendance to presidency. This is not an ideological or partisan group. There are no liberals or conservatives to us, just rich or poor—the strong or the weak. We support whoever provides us with the most money and potential for power. I've chosen the last five presidents and that's how we control the White House."

"You're prepping me to be your puppet president? No thank you, I have faith in the system."

"You're a strong man of principal, Mr. Coughlin. That's why you were my first choice to be president. Too bad you're overlooking the obvious.

"Which is?"

"You're already cozy in bed with us. It's been that way for a many, many years. My organization has funded your attorney general and gubernatorial campaigns. Elections aren't cheap and they're definitely not fair. Stop living in denial."

Robert purposefully cut the recruitment pitch short. "Governor, there's more donors for you to meet inside." His flustered speech added legitimacy to what Victor's had said.

"Is it true? Am I in bed with the mob or whatever they call themselves?"

"What do you want me to say? I believed in you when nobody in politics was willing to fork over the money. Your gubernatorial campaign was dead in the water until I worked out a deal to end the teacher's strike. I had to salvage it somehow."

"So, in your world the ends justify the means?"

"Yes, because I live in the real world. And who are you to judge my strategy? I'm the one who hides your indiscretions from the constituents, not to mention your family. You're an average politician who I transformed into a presidential hopeful. You need me as much as I need you."

"It's with good reason I had you sign the non-disclosure agreement. Clean out your office first thing in the morning. You're fired."

"You're firing me? You won't last a month on the campaign trail on your own."

When secrets are revealed it can rock a solid foundation to its core. Coughlin's fragile ego dismissed any possibility that his career was based on lies. The financial backing and backroom deals had more to do with his success than the politician was willing to admit. Governor Coughlin set off to prove the doubters wrong by becoming the President of the United States without the help of organized crime.

CHAPTER 20

RETALIATION

Five well-dressed Yakuza approached me in the parking lot of Baxter Studios. I was there to learn the basics of the filmmaking process. Instead, I was introduced to the seedy underbelly of Japan's criminal underworld. The Yakuza proposed a silent partnership, which was code for extortion. They had their hands in the pockets of every business except for the movie business and that had to change.

"You're not seeing the big picture here, Mr. Baxter. Porn is a growing business and we have young girls who can star in the films. That's on top of the security we're providing at an affordable cost. If you get in good with us you'll never have to worry about any mysterious "accidents.""

"Are you threatening me?"

"I'd say we're looking out for your best interests. You're an American and you don't understand how dangerous Tokyo can be at times. It's not how it used to be when I was a child."

"My company doesn't need any protection."

"I beg to differ. Wasn't your daddy killed a month or two ago? I have a feeling our services will be needed in the immediate future."

Yakuza thugs were gearing up to vandalize the Baxter Studios building. They'd held a grudge against my family since the studio released an embarrassing movie based on the gang. My team agreed to hold off on our campaign to focus on the Yakuza threat. First, we targeted an underground Pachinko casino owned by Masafumi Ono, a regional boss, known for his tight ponytail, red circular shades and gaudy jewelry.

After a week of surveillance, Denise recognized someone leaving the casino. She pointed out the woman from the passenger seat of my car.

"That's my aunt Sumie with those bodyguards. I wonder what she's doing here ? I bet she's doing undercover work, again."

"Undercover work? Why would Sumie Kaito be working undercover? There's obviously something you guys neglected to tell me," I said.

"Sumie Kaito is the assistant director of the PSIA. She has been a highly decorated intelligence agent for as long as I can remember."

Impulsively, I grabbed a duffle bag from the trunk of my car. I pulled out the skull mask and put it onto my face. It felt strange. I adjusted the harness to fit my head properly. Before I realized it, I was standing in front of the doors of the casino.

The people inside seemed to be in a hypnotic trance. Their eyes hardly ever strayed from the colorful slot machines. A man dressed in a black suit and white mask did not garner the attention I expected. Apparently, I wasn't interesting enough to compete with the constant bells and whistles. I had to do something impactful to show the Yakuza that I hadn't wandered in from a cosplay event.

An undercover cop tapped me on the shoulder and asked me to leave. Finally, I had caught the attention of one of the Yakuza's lackeys. I twisted his arm inward and snapped it at the elbow faster than he could react. Now, everyone in the casino understood I wasn't some drunk lunatic. My actions stole the spotlight and I used the platform to introduce myself to world."

"My name is ACE and I am here to send you guys a message. This city is under my protection for now on. Spread the word to your bosses. Tokyo is under new management, no more extortion. Does anyone have a problem with anything I've just said?" (No one said a word.)

Denise camped out near the front entrance to cover my exit. She was shocked by the believability of my new character.

"You changed as soon as you put on the mask. I did not recognize you when you were in there. It was almost as if your father had come back to life."

"I had to be scary believable to build my rep and to create chatter."

"Well, you certainly achieved your objective."

Back at HQ, the team held a brainstorming session on how to handle the Yakuza presented danger. Everyone traded ideas back and forth except for me. I, on the other hand focused on the most recent secret to be revealed.

"How in the hell did you forget to mention that you're sister's an intelligence agent."

"What? Where'd you get this information from?" Kenzan replied.

"I wasn't supposed to say anything without clearing it with Denise first. On our stakeout, we watched her come out of a casino and get into a black Mercedes."

"Sumie has been investigating the Yakuza throughout her storied career in the PSIA. Once they promoted her to the assistant director position she stopped working undercover. I haven't seen or spoken to her since she went off the grid."

"This beef between you guys, for whatever reason has gone on for too long. Jot down her address, I'm going there immediately."

"I guess we don't have a choice anymore. Hand me a pen and paper from the desk."

An hour later, I was welcomed into Sumie's spacious Tokyo apartment. She opened the door and said, "You are definitely your father's son...please come in." Sumie had a youthful face and vibrant personality. Her hair was cut short and her bangs highlighted those remarkably dark eyes.

I came inside and stretched out on the sofa loveseat. I caught a glimpse of the multicolored tattoo trailing her spine as she poured me a glass of cold water.

"I didn't expect to meet you so soon.... ugh..."

"It's Phillip, my name is Phillip," I replied.

"Oh nice…you're the third. Are you here about the flash drive, *Phillip*?"

"How do you know about the audio file?"

"A couple of months ago, a former CIA agent informed me of an incriminating flash drive. Your father couldn't give it to me personally without putting lives in danger."

"Do you know where Dad hid the flash drive? We haven't been able to find it."

"Yes, of course I do. Didn't Cole tell you where?"

"His memory is impaired, long story."

"The flash drive was kept in a lock box at your father's bank. The lawyer should've awarded it to you when he read the will," she said.

"What you're saying…it should be in my possession?"

"You didn't check the lock box they gave you?"

"No, at the time I wanted nothing from my dad."

"Your feelings are understandable based on the lies you were fed your whole life. Sometimes, family can hurt you more than your enemies and that's exactly what my brother did."

"What did Kenzan do to make you so upset?"

"I suspect my brother played a part in our parents' disappearance. We received a Black Hand letter that implied as much. I eventually joined the agency to gain access to their resources. I have to tell you—the Black Hand has been targeting you since you got here. They're framing you as the whistleblower that exposed the NSA. The other day, the FBI linked your IP address to the one that released the documents."

"You serious?"

"Dead serious. According to your profile, it makes perfect sense to tag you as a traitor. On the outside you appear to be a loner who grew up in a dysfunctional family. Both of your parents died a year apart from each other and you're emotionally vulnerable. Don't forget your dad renounced his American citizenship. Now you're seeking asylum here in Japan."

"What they're saying isn't true. I'm only here because of my father's funeral."

"The truth is subjective in the world of espionage. What matters is what you can prove. I've used my clout at the agency to block the CIA's investigation. It won't last if they can make a connection to the bombings. You have less than a week before they add you to the CIA's Most Wanted list."

The CIA ruined my life and then they branded me a traitor. What else could they take from me? Something drastic had to happen from our end. First, we had put our minds together and figure out their plan.

Sumie and I drove to the bank to recover the flash drive. The teller brought us the safety deposit box after I confirmed my identity. "Here you go, Mr. Baxter. I apologize for not believing you, sir. We have many safeguards in place to prevent fraud." The box only contained two items, the flash drive and a letter I had not read.

CHAPTER 21

TRUE COLORS

Sumie reunited with her brother for the first time in years. You could tell by the awkward silence between them. Neither one of them was sure of how to act or what to do. A natural divide developed from working on the opposite sides of the law. This divide played a major part in the dissolution of the family bond.

Cole assembled the team in the underground garage to listen to the decrypted audio. It horrified every last one of us to hear those evil men plotting JFK's death. I tried to decipher the Black Hand's ultimate goal once the team was up to speed.

Denise said, "They're deviating from their established patterns. There is a method to how they operate and there's no way they've changed overnight. You understand how history works, it repeats. Find the pattern in what they're doing."

"Let's list what we know about the syndicate. They're obsessed with money, power, wars...oh yeah and they're very sexist." I thought about it for a minute. "Um...I got it! The Black Hand has used fear to incite of the public fear for decades. They're killing two birds with one stone by releasing the documents. The bombings and the leaks are setting up their next "justified" war in the Middle East. At the same time the Black Hand is destroying my credibility to offset the impact of the audio file. The mystery is how they're pulling it off without getting caught."

Sumie recently resumed her cover as the on-and-off girlfriend of Masafumi Ono. "Masafumi has given me access to everything including his schedule. I'll show you how to get to him when he's the most vulnerable."

Masafumi's driver was taking him home when something heavy thumped onto the roof of the black Mercedes-Benz S-Class. The driver checked the rearview mirror, signaled and prepared to pull over. That's when a sword punctured, carved and rolled open the roof like a tuna can. I pulled Masafumi out the car and vanished into the cover of night.

We brought Masafumi to ACE headquarters under sedation. I tied him to a chair, arms behind the back and left the room to the interrogators.

During the interrogation, Cole played "good cop" to Denise's "bad cop." They played off each other's strengths masterfully. Cole's icy calm demeanor definitely made him out to be the reasonable one. Denise promised to do unspeakable things to him as he puffed his chest out in defiance.

She unsheathed a blade, untied Masafumi's left arm and placed it onto a table. Denise raised the blade high in the air and chopped off the tip of his pinky finger. "Aaaaahhhh!" He screamed uncontrollably. "You guys are a bunch of sadistic maniacs. Who are you people and where is the skull guy?"

Denise was prepared to do the same thing to the right hand. Cole, an expert on body language, thought she bluffed which is why he didn't intervene the first time.

"You're going to kill him before he gives up the

information." Cole said.

"I'm adhering to the strict code of the Yakuza. Masafumi disappointed us and must atone by losing the first joint of his finger." Denise fired back. "Open your eyes, man. It's kill or be killed in Tokyo."

"We're not supposed to be as bad as the Yakuza bosses. I won't be a part of this outfit if this is how we conduct ourselves."

"I'll step back…you can run this show, Mr. CIA."

Denise covered Masafumi's hand with a white towel. You could read the nervousness in his eyes while she provided the aid. Cole paced back and forth as he continued the line of questioning.

"What is your gang planning on doing to the Baxter Company?"

"I will not betray my family." Masafumi said.

"We have your girlfriend in the next room. My psychotic friend is willing to kill her if you won't talk. You've experienced enough today to know we're telling the truth." (Sumie screamed loudly)

"You won, okay. You won. I'll talk but have you promise to let us both go unharmed."

"Start talking and I'll give you my word," Cole said.

"We made a deal with the Black Hand to bomb the studio for them. We already hated the Baxter boy's father which was an added incentive."

"What else do you know?"

"Nothing, absolutely nothing."

We released Masafumi a couple of hours later and the local police picked him up soon after. A "concerned citizen" called in an anonymous tip.

"Cole promised he wouldn't do anything but I didn't," Denise said.

Cole was troubled by Denise's behavior during the interrogation. He confronted her immediately following the conclusion of our meeting. Cole began by describing his history of serving in the Middle East. He respectfully challenged the reasoning behind her actions. "The information gained through torture is unreliable. Not to mention the moral and ethical implications."

Denise reacted defensively, claiming he was overly sympathetic to criminals. "I got no sympathy for thugs. I reserve my sympathy for the victims and their families." Denise asked Cole to stay out of her way and she'd do the same for him.

"What was that about?" I asked.

"Denise and I were having a spirited debate on torture before you walked in."

"I appreciate you guys pretending to play nice but I'm not stupid. It's obvious you keep a healthy distance when possible. Is that why you don't come along on missions with us? I hope we don't make you feel uncomfortable."

"There is only one of us who's uncomfortable around Denise and it's not me. What's the story between you two anyway?" Cole said.

"I met Denise on campus my freshman year of college. She sat next to me in one of those required math classes and I fell madly in love. Suffice to say, it was all an elaborately constructed lie. It hurts to work with her every day but I have to carry on my family's mission."

"I can speak from personal experience as a former spy and field agent. Real emotions get mixed in with business...it's happened to me. You may not be the only one who's struggling with this partnership."

"Denise comes off as so strong and put together I often forget she's human."

"Keep an eye on her for both of our sakes. There's more going on with her than she's willing to let on."

Moments into the conversation, I received a text from Marise inviting me over for some drinks. This was the first time she invited me over to her house. I had to see Marise before the authorities got to me. I accepted her invitation as long as she granted me the honor of cooking for her. Marise sounded excited at the possibility of seeing me in the kitchen.

Against my better judgment, I showed up at Marise's home carrying a bouquet of flowers. She took my jacket at the door, placed the flowers in a vase and gave me a mini tour of the place. Marise had a lot of American furniture, which I asked her about. She mentioned that she lived there shortly with family. I wasn't aware of her past in America. She knew I was an American and didn't think it was important to mention that tidbit of information.

Marise left me in the kitchen to go to work. The centerpiece of the meal was my mom's world famous lasagna with garlic bread. The smell of my food made both of us hungry. I could have sworn her stomach growled. When the food was ready, I set the table and we finally ate. Marise thanked me for the meal and I thanked her for the nice kitchen to cook it in.

I'd been clearing the table until she said, "How would you like your desert?" Marise was sitting by the fireplace and requested my company. I scurried over to her corner of the room. "Aren't you going to kiss me?" Marise asked. I brushed back her hair gently, leaned in and my lips pressed softly against hers. Then everything went black...

CHAPTER 22

FEMME FATALE ATTRACTION

A pool of blood filled my mouth faster than I could spit it out. I had been blindfolded, undressed to my boxers and shackled to a wall. My futile efforts to break loose garnered an abundance of laughs. They fed me enough to keep me alive but not well enough to make me strong. My requests for answers were emphatically denied. "Who are you ladies? Why am I here? Is this the work of the Yakuza or the Black Hand?" All I knew was that somewhere out there my friends were extremely worried. They had to be searching everywhere. I wasn't the type of person to disappear without leaving at least a note.

I awaited my captor to make his or her intentions known. The last memory I had was my kiss with Marise. I asked one of the women if Marise was okay and if I could talk to her. "Marise is fine, you should be worrying about yourself, pretty boy." Her response angered me to my core. I demanded to speak to their boss. I wanted confirmation Marise was still alive. They whispered amongst themselves, then one of them left the room.

The door squeaked open. I smelled a familiar fragrance. Could it have been Marise? Did they bring her here to torture right before my very own eyes? I reacted like a mad man, pulling on the chains vigorously. My behavior agitated the woman in charge. I received two lashes of a whip in retaliation. "Take the blindfold off of him, right now!" I could spot Marise's soft yet confident voice anywhere. They removed the blindfold, my eyes gradually adjusted to the brightness of the light.

My sight confirmed my worst suspicion. Even though it was Marise, nothing about her was reminiscent of the woman I had come to know. She grabbed my face and stared directly into my eyes.

"Did you enjoy the kiss, baby? I hear my lipstick packs a potent punch," Marise said.

"Why did you do this to me? Are you an agent of Project ATLAS?" I replied.

Marise smiled while releasing my face. She walked out of the room and returned with an old photograph. In the picture, a cute little girl was sitting on Kenzan's lap. I had seen the picture before but I couldn't put my finger on it.

"My father shows everyone this picture from our photo album. I'm sure it's the same one he showed you the first time you came over to the house."

She revealed her true identity as Marise Kaito, the daughter of Kenzan. Her alias, Madam Karma AKA Widow Maker was hired by Project ATLAS to kill me. "If you're really Marise Kaito, the daughter of my Sensei, why are you trying to kill me? You're father wouldn't have allowed you to become a mercenary. This is a trick to mess with my mind—it's not going to work."

Marise and her father never saw eye to eye and things worsened in her teenage years. At 16, she ran away from her home. She lived on the streets for a while, doing any-and-everything for money. An older Japanese gentleman named Ryo Yoshida saw the beautiful young woman scrounging for food outside of a restaurant. He invited Marise to have dinner with him out of pity. They conversed about life and Marise shared her troubling family history. He offered her a job and a place to live. She accepted his offer and moved from the street into a mansion in just a few hours.

Ryo owned a massage parlor in the Sunset District of San Francisco. The parlor had been a front for an illegal brothel sponsored by the Yakuza. He trafficked young girls from Asian countries such as Vietnam, Singapore and Thailand to be prostitutes. Ryo supplied the girls with shelter, drugs and arranged the appointments. The "Johns" came in for their "massage" and handpicked their favorite from a lineup of women.

The demeaning selection process created a competitive atmosphere in the brothel. More work meant higher compensation and better living. The older women were coerced into outdoing the younger girls who moved into the home. Marise received instant hate because she was a highly sought-after worker and Ryo's favorite. She had been the only one given permission to live in Ryo's mansion instead of the boarding house.

In the 5 years at the brothel, Marise suffered physical and emotional abuse at the hands of Ryo and the Johns. Marise started cutting her wrists to avert attention from the emotional pain. The visible scars were not good for business and eventually Ryo fitted her in elbow length gloves to hide the forearms.

The men paid Marise tons of money to fulfill their perverted Japanese bondage fantasies. When the lights dimmed, the confident commanding "Karma" flipped the switch and Marise played the role to perfection.

Marise would've killed to return to the days of eating dinner with her family or training at her father's dojo. She considered running home to her family countless times. They'd be so ashamed of what had become of their daughter.

A new Thai girl named, Sophee moved into the boarding house. Marise oriented her on the realities of the business. They formed a close relationship though language was sometimes a barrier. On a summer evening, one of the Johns complained about Sophee's service. Ryo raised his hand to her as an example to the other girls. When Marise saw Sophee threatened, it awakened something deep inside her. She removed her stiletto shoe and stabbed him in the eye in front of all the prostitutes.

"Ladies, you know me as Marise and sometimes as Karma. For too long I've hurt myself and made myself weak when it should have been men to feel my wrath. We've been going about our business the wrong way. These men come in here begging for domination. They show their true heart's desire. Our society tells men they should be in charge. They are afraid to admit that they want us women to dominate them. We're much stronger than we've shown and if you follow me, together we'll bring enlightenment to our world." On that day, Marise resurrected herself as Karma, the madam of the house.

Madam Karma assumed control of the brothel's business. She gave the prostitutes the option of leaving or staying to work for her. The Kabukis as she called them, found a place at Madam Karma's massage parlor. She trained them in martial arts and gave them purpose. She taught the women to treat every man as an object to manipulate. "Men have power and use this power to tilt the balance in their favor. I want to live in a world where women set the rules and the men have to manage." In this world, Marise was valued for her brains as much as she was valued for her beauty.

Marise clearly wasn't going to provide me a quick death. She went out of her way to keep me alive when she could have killed me. As Madam Karma she enjoyed inflicting pain on others far too much to limit her fun.

She revealed her master plan of throwing us an elaborate wedding. And after the wedding, she reserved the right to make herself a widow. "Till death do us part, Phil." I promised Marise in some way, shape or form she would pay for what she'd done. She pointed out my bad luck with women, just to spite me. Marise pointed out that both of my last girlfriends lied and manipulated me. Her words definitely had an effect on me in my vulnerable state.

"Do you know why I call my warriors Kabukis?"

"Because they're whores and prostitutes, kind of like the original actors in the Kabuki plays."

"Watch your wretched tongue you cretin. As I was saying, the name is inspired by a day out at the Noh theatre I had with your father. To be honest, I thought the plays were boring. They're too traditional for my tastes. Luckily, I discovered Kabuki theaters and loved them. It's more modern and edgy. The actors don't wear masks. They wear makeup to enhance their natural beauty. I don't hide behind a mask like your father did. I can't separate who I am from what I do."

I hurled blood-filled saliva onto her white leather bodysuit.

"It's bad luck to see each other so close to the

wedding. Bad luck for you, mostly. You're lucky I have to change into my wedding dress anyway."

"It's true what they say about karma because you're definitely a bit--." That's all I got out before I was gagged.

Marise made the mistake of sending a wedding invitation to Kenzan's address. She wanted her father to be there to walk her down the aisle and unwittingly gave my team the information they needed to rescue me. "Cheer up Phil! You should be happy we're combining our two families." She paused. "I might just keep you around and quit my job. You never know what I might do. I did enjoy those dates we went out on."

None of Marise's comments could be taken with a grain of salt besides the reference to her favorite weapon, the katana. "I love the katana. It's elegant and curved—comparable to a woman." Truthfully, her mind was her most dangerous weapon. "I'm the one who broke into Denise's home two months ago...needed something borrowed for the wedding. I already had something old, new and blue so I "borrowed" the serpent charm from Denise."

Marise promised to return it to her after the ceremony.

I could have played into her hands as she expected me to do. The truth is I've matured since coming to Japan. My perspective on life had changed. I understood that if I played my cards right I could throw her off her game. I shouted, "I know you're not going to wear white to the wedding. You better wear black…you're far from pure."

She lunged at me with a small blade but one of the Kabukis managed to stop her. I rattled her nerves, something she did not think possible. The Kabukis took her away to get ready for the ceremony. My insults earned me another few extra minutes of punishment from these fierce women warriors. An average man would have already died from the loss of blood. The meditation techniques I learned were probably the only reason I survived.

The Kabukis groomed me for the upcoming nuptials. They lowered my shackles, dressed me in a tuxedo, and escorted me out of the changing room. I walked down a decorated hallway at sword-point. I recognized memorabilia from several iconic movie scenes. By some means, Madam Karma had commandeered the Baxter Studios' main office as her base. Madam Karma retained a number of the female staff to operate the equipment and to film the documentary.

The Kabukis chained me to the ground as they completed the last minute preparations. They positioned Tungsten and LED lights around the set to enhance the filming aesthetics. Once they completed that task, the Kabukis added a small table in the front of the room near the altar. I objected to the use of makeup, nonetheless they applied the cosmetics. A tall woman jammed a camera in my face for a close-up angle. I swatted her back though the chains restricted my movement. "I don't understand why you're complaining. Guys usually love Madam Karma's movies. The content of the movies are usually less PG. Come to think of it, I do recognize the chains. We're just missing the whip."

CHAPTER 23

DADDY'S GIRL

At Kenzan's home, a suspicious letter had been included in his mail. He unsealed the envelope, removed a card and read it. Kenzan was invited to the wedding of ACE and Madam Karma. He implored Denise, Cole and Sumie to meet with him even though there was a major storm raging outside. The sky turned black and the wind howled like a wolf on a full moon. He waited for them at the door. Denise came in soaking wet, looking less than picture perfect. He held the invitation up to her face and she took a few moments to read it.

"Who is Madam Karma and why is she marrying PBIII? Is this some type of joke?"

"She's my daughter."

"It can't be my niece." Sumie said. "I've been investigating Madam Karma for a very long time. Her deeds are well documented in the global crime community."

Denise confided in Kenzan a lot over the years they'd known each other. He knew things about her, which no one else knew. She lived with Marise and loved her like a sister. He should've told her that her sister was a mercenary. Marise had the same training as ACE, technically more. She had knowledge of where they lived and where they taught. Denise's life was unknowingly put in danger every day. Kenzan had every right to keep certain things personal but not to this extent.

Sumie recounted the stories circulating in the mercenary underground about the Widow Maker. "There's no assassin more feared than Madam Karma. She's been all over the world murdering and mutilating her victims. She doesn't kill because she gets paid to do it; the money is just an added bonus. Her modus operandi consists of killing only men in the most violent ways possible. Her weapon of choice is the katana but she is adept at anything with a blade. She doesn't use firearms. They're not personal enough."

Madam Karma burst on to the scene a couple of years ago with abilities that rivaled my father's. That's when the phone calls flooded Kenzan's home inquiring whether he had trained this new assassin. Kenzan was adamant of fact that he never trained her or even met her. Madam Karma had skill but not the character he ingrained into his students. Kenzan waited for the day when Madam Karma and ACE crossed paths.

With relative ease, she moved into the number 3 spot on the mercenary pecking order. Marise's unstable personality prevented her from being seen as legitimate competition to ACE. Her clients put up with her eccentric behavior because of her unique talents. ACE's status as number 1 had been accepted for so long that the Black Hand feared he would grow unmanageable. Empowering another assassin besides ACE allowed them to maintain their stranglehold on the targeted killing business.

Her tactics appeared bizarre in comparison to ACE's. He was covert and she was overt. Marise's style went against everything developed through the Card System. Her psychopathic need to punish men threatened to undermine the establishment.

On her downtimes, Madam Karma moonlighted as a wedding crasher. At a typical crashed wedding, Madam Karma ties up and gags the bride. She disrobes the bride and puts on the dress. Madam Karma impersonates the bride and walks down the aisle. When the groom raises the veil he discovers it's not his bride and is stabbed in the heart. On other occasions, Madam Karma infiltrates the reception and kills every man in attendance. She doesn't kill boys because she doesn't consider them men yet.

You can imagine the type of psychological trauma she inflicts on her victims. The women are left to pick up the pieces of the lives without their husbands, sons, fathers and brothers. Madam Karma must believe she is helping them in her warped mind. Unfortunately for these victims, she is doing the complete opposite. "Someone must have done a number on her and she's taking it out on the rest of the male population."

"Her story can't be understood from the middle, Sumie. I have to start from the beginning." Kenzan said.

When Dad started his company, he couldn't do it alone. While he was busy killing world leaders and investment bankers, Kenzan was enrolled in college studying cinematography. On his own he learned how to build sets and conduct casting calls. Kenzan met a beautiful woman named, Lynn at a casting call and didn't pursue a relationship. He believed that dating one of the actresses had the potential to get messy. As time went on it was obvious they were attracted to each other. Lynn proposed a non-date, which could technically work around the company's dating policy. It would be two friends hanging out and eating some food. Kenzan agreed and after two years of not dating they got married.

Two years into the marriage, Kenzan and Lynn had their first child, Marise. Marise was troubled, even from a very young age. She was hardheaded and unwilling to follow her parents' instructions. Every afternoon, Marise returned from school sore from the disciplinary action taken by the teachers. She contested her teachers to the point of disrupting the entire class. They take education very serious in Japan and her behavior was not tolerated.

Lynn dealt with Marise the most because she did not work. Kenzan spent the bulk of his time at the studio. She worried about her parenting skills and thought of herself as a failure. None of the other children in the village acted like this. Where did she go wrong? She tried punishing, rewarding, smothering and ignoring and nothing worked for this child. When Kenzan invited Denise to live at his home it made things even worse.

Denise was an angel; her respectful attitude gained her favor in Kenzan's eyes. Lynn complimented Denise excessively and used her as the measuring stick for Marise. Marise despised her sister because of the perceived favoritism. Denise, on the other hand did not understand the root of the discord.

Marise grew tired of taking care of her "perfect" sibling. Denise understandably encountered set backs while adjusting to a new life and the loss her birth parents. Kenzan relied on Marise to be their unofficial babysitter and support. Marise had to take Denise to the market with her when she ran errands and let Denise tag along when she played with her friends.

When Marise traveled throughout the village, the elders always reprimanded her. They said she had evil spirits in her. The Kaito's neighbor, Mr. Sato was the worst offender. He was the first to call her a demon-child and turned the others against her. Marise reached out to Denise who wasn't yet astute in the matters of life to give useful advice.

Mr. Sato came home one day from work and found 3 dead cats hanging from the ceiling lamp in his living room. The unbearable stench caused his eyes to water. He opened the windows to ventilate the room and disposed of the cats. Moments later, he stomped furiously to his neighbor's home to confront the Kaito parents. Lynn was disturbed by the allegation but she defended her daughter. He had no evidence to prove Marise's involvement. Nonetheless, she talked to both of the girls about it. "You girls have to think and act purely, it affects your karma. Your thoughts, actions and words, not only follow you in this life but the next."

Marise didn't deny it. She saw nothing wrong with her actions. Lynn's every worst nightmare had been realized in that conversation. Marise described the incident with a blank emotionless affect. Lynn forced her daughter to keep her mouth shut and to never speak of it again.

Kenzan reflected on the way he had handled things and opted for a change. He asked for some time off and a reduced his work schedule so he could focus on Marise. With more time on his hands, Kenzan reopened his dojo to train to his daughter. When he informed Marise of the training she moaned and complained incessantly. Marise believed Kenzan overreacted to the hanging cats incident. To soften the blow, Kenzan included Denise in the training to make it seem less like a punishment and more like a rite of passage.

The first few days of training were rough. The

concept of patience was foreign to Marise. She wanted to beat people up and do flashy kicks from the beginning. That's not the main benefit of what martial arts offers. His objective was to build up her human vessel through consistent work and patience. For weeks, they only meditated, stretched and talked. Combining Kenzan's two loves—his family and teaching filled him with boundless joy. Denise benefitted greatly from the increased attention she received from her father. Her new dream was to take over the dojo when Kenzan retired. Kenzan was prouder than he had ever been in his life.

Denise's improvement starkly contrasted with the maturation process of her older sister. Marise hadn't absorbed the teachings at the speed everyone would have hoped. Kenzan had no desire to giving up on his daughter. Lynn's patience wore thin after years trying to keep her family together. Slowly but surely, a glimmer of hope sprang out of a sea of pessimism. Lynn received a call from Marise's teacher stating how much her grades and behavior had improved. Kenzan took credit insisting the improvement be attributed to his teachings. Lynn agreed. She anticipated what new fortunes the future would bring.

Things had been at a much better place than even Marise believed possible. Unfortunately, she couldn't leave well enough alone. The girls had graduated from hand-to-hand combat to weapons training. After one of the practices, Marise continued to spar with her sister. (Kenzan's students sparred with wooden Bokken swords until they were proficient enough to advance to the real thing.) While they sparred, Marise asked Denise to close her eyes. When she opened them, she looked upon her father's most prized antique katana. Denise was scared, knowing that only trouble would come of this.

211

"I'm going to use this sword for something. Don't tell Dad."

"Dad hates when his things are misplaced, especially the dangerous weapons. What are you going to do with the sword, anyway?"

"I can't tell you what's up my sleeve. It's just something that I have to do. "

Denise ran home and told her father what Marise was up to. Kenzan and Lynn searched everywhere and couldn't find her. They stopped by their house and heard Mr. Sato yelling at the top of his lungs. Kenzan instructed the ladies to go inside their home and to wait for him. He opened the door to Mr. Sato's home and walked-in on Marise pointing the sword in their neighbor's direction. Mr. Sato was backed into a corner, fearing for his life.

Kenzan commanded her to put the sword down but for some reason she wouldn't do it. He calmly walked towards her from the front entrance. When Kenzan got within close proximity, he placed his hand on Marise's shoulder. She slowly lowered the katana then inexplicably swung the sword in her father's direction. Kenzan barely had space or time to evade her attack. He leaned backwards, saving his eye from damage. Nevertheless, the blade left a large gash on his face.

Marise had crossed a serious line, a line her father could not overlook. They had used every option at their disposal without concrete results to speak of. Lynn asked her family in the states if Marise could go to live with them. Lynn's cousin was apprehensive at first; she had her own issues to deal with. Plus she heard plenty about

Marise over the years.

After a few days to think, Lynn's cousin agreed that a fresh start could do her some good. Marise had burned every bridge in her life except for the ones in America. Denise was terrified of her sister and wouldn't be alone in the same room. Marise blamed her for running to her father and stopping from attacking Mr. Sato. Kenzan paid Mr. Sato a lot of money to keep the story quiet from the community. They sent her off to America and with this move ensured her a new beginning. Not long after moving to San Francisco, she ran away from her cousins' home and that's how she became Madam Karma.

When word reached back that Marise had run away, Lynn blamed her husband. It pained Kenzan to know his daughter was somewhere out on the streets. Lynn distanced herself from her husband and eventually divorced him. She tried to take Denise with her but she didn't want to go. Lynn left for America and Kenzan stayed to run the movie studio. Kenzan filled his spare time with teaching as a way to keep his mind off of his family. My dad empathized with Kenzan who was now in the same position he'd been in. Their strong friendship was the only thing, which kept them sane.

CHAPTER 24

'TIL DEATH

I had the misfortune of meeting Sophee for the first time, minutes before the commencement of the ceremony. Madam Karma delegated her the responsibility of officiating the wedding. The stylists dressed her in a black silk kimono, giant wig and heavy makeup. Madam Karma planned a contemporary Japanese style wedding, which combines Christian and traditional Japanese customs.

Strangely, I had a gang of butterflies fluttering about in my stomach. "Let me go. You know what she's doing is wrong. I'm aware of what's happened to you ladies but this not the proper course of action."

"Madam Karma is my mentor, hero and best friend. You should thank the heavens for the blessings rained down on your ungrateful head. Oh, if I were to be so lucky."

"You're sick in the head just like her! I would gladly trade places if you can make it happen."

The ceremony was scheduled to begin within minutes. Sophee proudly stood in front of the Shinto altar in anticipation of the bride. Madam Karma failed to walk down the aisle on time. After a few minutes, everyone wondered what had held her up. Victor had phoned Madam Karma for an update on the hit. He paid for my death, not for a reality show wedding. The longer I stayed alive the more danger I posed for the evil cabal. He ordered Madam Karma to end the theatrics and to perform her duty. If she maintained her current trajectory she would only serve as a foil to his plans.

Madam Karma ignored Victor's warning and resumed the ceremony. Her eyes stayed fixated on the clock. Kenzan didn't have the decency to show up and ruin the wedding. Madam Karma signaled for the processional music and walked down the aisle by her lonesome. She had on a racy wedding dominatrix outfit. Madam Karma wore a white leather corset, garter stocking and sheer veil. Her face, full of despair, sulked as she interlocked her arms with mine.

Sophee bowed to us and proceeded with the ceremony.

"My fellow Kabukis, we are gathered here today to celebrate the union between Marise Kaito and Phillip Baxter III. Marise, I have never seen you look as beautiful as you do right now. You deserve all the happiness in the world. I am proud to call you my dearest friend." She waved a branch from a sacred tree, signifying purification.

The Kabukis initiated the San-San-Kudo ritual. Traditionally, the bride and groom are served sake from three different ceramic cups. The groom sips three times from the first ceramic cup. The bride follows. The same process happens in reverse with the second cup. The ritual ends when the bride, groom and parents sipping from the third cup.

The wedding maidens brought the sake to our table on a wooden tray. I refused to participate. Sophee sucked her teeth in disgust. She announced, "If anyone can show just cause why this couple cannot be legally joined in marriage, let them speak now or forever hold their peace."

A loud crashed averted our attention from the nuptials. My eyes trailed a smoke bomb canister rolling across the floor. The emission of smoke obscured everyone's vision. A figure grabbed me, covered my face with a gas mask and unlocked my chains. I was directed out of the room and into one of the offices on the floor. A leather-clad Denise had pulled me out of the line of fire.

"We're lucky we got to you in time. Marise could've been the new Mrs. Baxter."

"You jealous?"

"Hardy-har-har! You should be kissing my feet for saving you, not cranking out jokes. The smoke is dissipating, we should locate our crew." On our way out of the room, Denise handed me my real mask and a katana. "Ready, ACE?"

Denise and I returned to the set where Kenzan, Sumie and Cole defended themselves against a horde of Madam Karma's warriors. Cole was inches away from being decapitated when Kenzan swooped in to save him. We ran to their aid to even up the odds. A vicious brawl ensued. The Kabukis attacked in a highly organized semi-dance formation. They waved razor-tipped folded hand fans, demonstrating a host of acrobatic maneuvers.

The Kabukis' primary objective was to incapacitate Denise. Sophee snatched her by the back of the head and smashed it into a camera. She threw Denise onto the ground and climbed on top of her. "I pity you, Denise. Madam Karma considered you a sister and you betrayed her. You have no idea what Mr. Sato did to her." Sumie pushed Sophee off of her and then Denise knocked her out with a spinning backhand.

Madam Karma escaped through a small corridor. I chased her down the stairs to the emergency exit door and cornered her.

"Stop Marise! Let's settle this right now, just you and I."

"You saw what I did to my father's face. What do you think I'll do to you?"

Madam Karma unsheathed her sword. I mirrored her by doing the same. Our blades collided; sparks flew like fireworks. She attacked aggressively with an overhand strike, I parried. I used my obvious strength advantage to push her onto her heels.

"It appears we're at an impasse," I said.

"Only if you think I'm out of tricks," Madam Karma replied.

Meanwhile, the sheer number of their opponents had overcome the team. I had to choose between my friends' lives and getting revenge. I chose friendship over revenge and sprinted in the other direction. I allowed Marise to escape, some things are more important than my desire for revenge. I turned the momentum of the battle in our favor. We defeated at least half of the Kabukis and their confidence depleted.

Madam Karma crept back into the battle without any of us noticing. While my back was turned, she lunged her sword at my abdomen. Denise telegraphed it and pushed me out of the way. Madam Karma impaled her in the stomach.

I caught Denise's body in midair and held her in my arms. Kenzan looked at his daughter absent of speaking a word. He rushed over to Denise's side. Marise heckled, "She can never be me or take my spot. I will never let that happen, father." The Kabukis dispersed.

"Cole, bring the car around now. Sumie, help him take her to the car. Kenzan and I will deal with this." I looked at Denise in her fragile condition and I thought of how much I loved her. I remembered how hurt I was when I found out she had been lying to me. "Denise, can you hear me? I love you, okay. Don't die, please don't die."

Denise replied, "I may not have much time, I want to say I never meant to hurt you." A tear rolled down her cheek, I softly wiped it off with my right thumb. "Don't cry Denise, you're going to live through this. We're going to hash all of this out."

"Ahem," Madam Karma cleared her throat. I returned my attention to her. She got into her fighting stance. I charged at her full speed. Madam Karma sidestepped my unfocused assault. My head was clearly someplace else. I thrust forward with my sword, dislodging the sword from her hand. Madam Karma executed a textbook crescent kick and I stumbled. Her swift kick knocked the taste out of my mouth. She tried it a second blow and I dodged it.

I raised the katana and pointed it to her throat.

"Do it! Just end it, end it for me," she said.

"Why Marise? That's the easy way out and I'm not going to do it for you," I replied.

Kenzan put himself in-between Madam Karma and the blade. "Talk to me for once my daughter. What happened to you? Can you answer me this?"

"You are so blind. Do you really not know? Mr. Sato, h-h-he molested me. More than once when I was six years old."

"Why didn't you tell me or your mother? Please help me to understand."

"This wouldn't have happened if you ever came home at a decent hour or if you paid any attention to your family. You're supposed to be my father. You're supposed to be my protector. You let Mr. Sato spread nasty lies about me, adding insult to injury. Ultimately, when I acted up you found my replacement. "

"Sorry, dear. You have to believe I'm sorry. That doesn't excuse what you've done. You can still make it right."

I threw in my own set of questions. "What's Victor's plan? When does it go into effect? I know he hired you to kill me. Give me something I can use against him." She didn't respond. "If you felt anything real for me, you would tell me how to stop them," I pleaded.

"The Black Hand wants to launch the next World War. In wartime, the CIA has more leeway to exercise its power. The government can use drones to eliminate whoever is deems a threat. They can even hold terrorists indefinitely. To start this war, Project ATLAS hired my Kabukis to steal intelligence from government officials. Victor arranged for the girls to meet politicians at their hotel rooms. My Kabukis gave them a good time and at the end of the night, the girls detonated the bombs."

"What a devious plan. Even if someone suspected something they can't come forward without exposing the politicians as a cheater. Which brings me to my next question. Who's the current target?"

"The Governor of Philadelphia, Fredrick Coughlin. The hit goes down sometime at the end of this week."

"Isn't he the guy my mom helped to put into office?"

"Yes, he's on the outs with the Black Hand for not "playing ball."

"Can't you call it off? The girls do work for you."

"Once the girls accept a contract I can't call it off. There's a no cancellation clause. It wouldn't be good business."

Cole and Sumie carried Denise's injured body to the car. The bumpy driving caused Denise to regain consciousness. She asked Sumie where they were going. Sumie told her not to speak and to conserve her energy. She feared Denise would bleed out. "We're almost there," Cole shouted from the driver's seat.

At the hospital, we waited in the emergency room. We were told Denise would be taken in for surgery. I couldn't shake an eerie feeling, being in the hospital for the first time since my mother's accident. Hospitals are cold, sterile and embody sickness. I remembered sitting by Mom's bed, holding her hand in the final days. Mom acknowledged her imminent death and maximized her limited time on earth. She told me she was proud to be my mother and blessed to have raised a strong man.

I prayed in the waiting room for hours. I asked God to give Denise a better outcome than my mother's. Denise was one of the strongest people I'd ever known. I couldn't bear to see another wonderful woman die before her time. I had left so many things unsaid. I kicked myself for taking time for granted.

Kenzan criticized me for unintentionally creating the whole debacle. "You're keeping secrets from your team time, now? You used to be the only one of us who didn't lead a double life. Now, you're the one who's creating costumes and withholding information. It's a slippery slope. Don't be in such a hurry to make the same mistakes as your dad."

"I messed up. I know that. I should've been upfront about my relationship. I thought the truth might hurt Denise. What's even worse is that Marise turned out to be a mercenary and your daughter."

"As a father, I must say I failed to protect my daughter. There were signs...clues I didn't picked up. What she is, who she turned out to be...she is my karma."

"You can't blame yourself for the rest of your life. The good in your life has outweighed the bad. Moving on is the only thing a sane person can do. Accepting suffering doesn't equate to accepting unhappiness."

The surgeons performed a successful surgery. They said the blade missed both of the intestines. They returned the serpent charm they found clenched in her fist. "I have to say, your friend is lucky to have survived. I'd classify it as a medical miracle. Must be this lucky charm," the doctor said.

The nurse allowed us only a few minutes to talk to her. I let Kenzan go first because he had a lot to say. The guilt of knowing his daughter did this to her, tore him up inside. When the time had almost run out, I inserted my head into the hospital room. Denise invited me in and Kenzan gave us privacy.

"I can't believe I had to thank Cole for saving my life. He's not going to let me live this down. I have to thank you too."

"I should be thanking you. More importantly, I should be telling you what's in my heart. I love you, Denise. Rarely does a guy get the chance to fall in love twice with the same person. The woman you really are is even more impressive than the girl you pretended to be."

"I heard you when you said it the first time. I love you too. Not to dampen the moment but you have to see this."

She turned on the evening news. My face was plastered all over it. A Syrian man claiming to be Amed Hammoud released a video proclaiming to be the mastermind behind the bombings. He named me as an accomplice and most trusted disciple. Hammoud took credit for essentially paralyzing the U.S. government. No elected officials showed up to work after another rash of bombings. "Your children are afraid to attend their schools, your leaders are hiding underground. Planes are going to fall out of the sky next, if your President doesn't give in to my demands."

"You have to go into hiding. Someone in this hospital might recognize you as the man from the news. Go. I'll be fine, okay."

"I can't leave now, you need me. There's nowhere to run, it's over. They're even rubbing my nose in it by involving my grandpa's old cover identity.

"The team is here to take care of me. We've sacrificed our lives to complete this mission. You're the wild card, the ace in the hole. You won't lose."

I gave her a peck on the forehead. She grabbed my arm, placed the serpent charm in my palm and closed it. I nodded my head and she smiled. As soon as I came out of her room, people started whispering. I speed walked through the hallway and used the staircase to get out of there.

I had kept a facial prosthetic kit and false identification in the car. I put on a new face and abandoned the car on the side of the road. I scheduled a flight and rode the express train to the Narita Airport. I got through security without a problem. I flew back to my home state of Philadelphia a week and a half before Thanksgiving.

CHAPTER 25

ROOM SERVICED

Governor Coughlin had built his brand on wholesome family values. His philandering lifestyle was no secret in the political circles though. The Governor's marriage only existed to support Fredrick's political ambitions. Claudine, his wife tested well with the female demographic and adopted a busy schedule of her own. The day I started tailing them, she had attended one of their children's soccer games and the governor had flown to DC to raise campaign money.

In Washington, it was business as usual for the most part. On day two, he deviated from his official schedule. Fredrick gave the secret service the day off even though it wasn't advised. He checked in under a pseudonym, at an extravagant hotel in the outskirts of the capital. Fredrick received the keys and went to his room where he anxiously awaited his prostitute. He picked up the phone and dialed his wife.

"Hey honey, how's the game going? Did Jackson score a goal?"

"We won! And Jackson scored the game-winning goal! I'm so proud of him. I wish you could've seen it."

"I know...I wish I didn't have to be away during the season. Tell Jackson I'm proud of him and I can't wait to congratulate him in person."

"I'll do that."

"I have to go, I have an important meeting in the morning."

"Okay. I love you and I'll speak to you tomorrow."

"Love you too."

Fredrick made a second call to the escort service. He informed them of the room number and confirmed the agreed upon time. "Yes, this is Client 5. I've checked into the hotel. Sapphire should have no trouble getting to my room. I'm in suite number 653."

A young Asian prostitute entered the hotel lobby and took the elevator to the 6th floor. Sapphire stepped out of the elevator and searched for the correct room. She stopped in front of Room 653 and rang the bell twice. Fredrick opened the door, greeted her and closed the door behind her.

"Do you speak English? The last girl didn't speak any English. You better speak English or come with a hot translator."

"Yes, sir. I do speak English."

"Excellent. What else do you do?"

Sapphire removed her oversized trench coat. Fredrick reached his hand out to touch and she slapped his hand. She led him by the hands into the bedroom. Sapphire ripped off his clothes and handcuffed him to the headboard of the bed. She gagged him with his own tie and went into the other room. Sapphire unlocked Fredrick's briefcase and photographed the documents.

Minutes after, she returned with an explosive vest. Fredrick's eyes bulged. He attempted to break free of the cuffs. The young prostitute calmed him down by injecting a mild sedative into the side of Fredrick's neck. "You're going to be assassinated before you're sworn into presidency." She kissed him on the forehead. "Oh the irony."

A bellboy knocked on the door.

Sapphire ignored the loud noise.

The bellboy continued to pound.

Sapphire put on a robe and answered the door.

"Excuse me ma'am, your neighbors complained of strange noises coming out of your suite. It's an elderly couple next door who is trying to sleep."

"My boyfriend and I are very passionate. Some might say "explosive." I assure you, the couple will have no problems sleeping tonight."

"One more thing..." The bellboy tilted his head forward and sprayed a green mist out of his mouth. It wasn't really a bellboy; it was I in a disguise. I subdued Sapphire and threw her onto the bed next to the governor. I retrieved her mini camera and captured the moment digitally. Fredrick came to just as I snapped the final photo.

"Am I dead?"

"Don't let the skull mask fool you, you're still alive."

"What's with the flashes of light?"

"I was taking pictures of you, handcuffed to a bed, next to a prostitute."

"Why are you doing this to me? Don't you know I'm running for president? I have a family."

"Should've thought of that before you booked a room at this hotel. You cheated on your wife, you cheated death but you're not going to cheat the country. Your presidential bid is over."

The Governor lost support from his rich donors once the pictures were released. His wife had no incentive to stick around since he had no shot at being president. More pictures surfaced and opportunist hookers cashed in on their fifteen minutes of fame. Coughlin's political career appears to be over but Americans love a comeback story.

CHAPTER 26

HOUSE OF CARDS

Going home was out of the question. The FBI had snipers planted on rooftops and agents on the ground. Dad owned a safe house in the southern part of the city. I stayed there undetected for a couple of days.

Someone softly knocked on the door. I removed my gun and looked through the peephole. It was a harmless older woman or so it seemed. "Who are you?" I yelled through the door. "It's Aunt Jo," she replied. Her face matched a picture from the photo album. I unlocked the deadbolt, unlatched the chain lock and invited her inside. I gave her a warm hug once she dropped her bags onto the table.

"What are you doing here? How did you find me?"

"Your friend, Denise contacted me. She created me a new identity so I could travel here without being detained. Denise planned on surprising you for Thanksgiving."

"I read about you in my dad's journal. He described how much you cared for him. You were the closet thing he had to a mother."

"I loved him so much, we lost touch when he went back to Japan. If I had known about you, I would've been there. No more dwelling on the past. You shouldn't have to go another year without your aunt on the holidays."

Thanksgiving was once my least favorite holiday. The emphasis on big families and togetherness soured me on the day. I had no close relationships with any of my cousins, aunts, uncles or grandparents. Well, not until I met Aunt Jo on that Thanksgiving. She embodied the meaning of the holiday and the fulfillment of family.

Aunt Jo whipped up a nice home-cooked meal. The awesome aroma caused my mouth to water. We held hands and prayed over the steaming food. Aunt Jo shared how thankful she was to know the truth. The strange behavior exhibited by the men in my family finally made sense to her.

Aunt Jo asked me to say what I was thankful for. "I'm thankful for you, Aunt Jo. This was such an unexpected surprise."

I enjoyed the stuffing, turkey and mash potatoes etc. I shared my impression of the meal. "This is delicious. I haven't eaten like this in since my mom was alive." I asked Aunt Jo to stay at the house until I returned. She was scared to let me go. "Be careful, nephew."

When Dad died a few months ago, I thought I was going to a regular funeral. Since then, I learned the totality of my life had been based on lies. Over and over again the universe taught me not to trust a cute girl with a smile. Well that's not true. I found out that I could trust a few people and together we formed a team. The biggest lesson was not to judge people so quickly. The journals shattered my perceptions of who I believed my parents to be.

That's why I felt a rush when I stepped onto the grounds of the High Rollers Casino in Philly. I had the opportunity to confront the one and only, Victor Rinaldi.

He needed to explain why he did what he did to my face. I wanted to taste his fear as he stared down the barrel of a gun.

In the casino, I rubbed elbows with the experienced gamblers at the roulette table. It was imperative for me to maintain a low profile while I surveyed the room. I mingled with some guests, inquiring whether the owner made frequent appearances. Victor was rarely seen in any of his casino except for this one. This casino was special to him because its distinction of being the original. It symbolized his rise from the son of a gangster to the leading member of the Commission.

I wrestled some information out of one of the cocktail waitresses who saw Victor leave through the rear exit earlier in the evening. She believed he would likely return before the night had ended.

Breaking into the Rinaldi Suite without getting caught was harder than anticipated. A man with secrets keeps them well guarded. I devised a plan, which included the implementation of card counting. Card counting is not illegal. It is heavily frowned upon in casinos though. The strategy gives players a rare advantage and casinos hate that. The players who get caught are usually hassled and kicked out.

For the system to work, a card counter must be able to recognize when he has an advantage. I lost a couple of hands then hit my stride. Instantly, a hyped group of women encircled the table to cheer me on.

The Game Manager monitored my activities from the backroom. He singled me out on the multiple camera screens. I tripled my starting amount of forty thousand and the security guards pulled me out of the game. The gigantic bodyguards ushered me into the back where the Game Manger threatened harm.

The two security guards towered on both sides of the Game Manager. Their laughable intimidation tactics fell flat on me. They boasted that the room was soundproof amongst other things. "You come back to this casino again and I'll break your legs, personally. This is not a request. It's a warning. Capeesh!"

I flung a throwing knife into the throat of the guard on the left. I charged at him and reached for the gun in his shoulder holster. *Bang!* Shot him in the head. *Bang!* The guard on the other side died too.

A downward blood trail adorned the wall. The Game Manger started making deals to save his life. I snatched him up by the back of his neck, demonstrating real intimidation.

"You're going to let me into your bosses office, capeesh!"

"I-I-I caaaan't do that. He'll kill me."

"There's literally nothing to stop me from killing you right now. If you lead me to Victor I'll consider you on the side of angels this one time."

"Chill out. I got the key to the office. I'm cooperating, remember I'm cooperating."

Victor entered his office and dropped his keys on to the coffee table. He removed his jacket and hung it up on the rack. He could detect another being in the room. I turned in the executive chair to face him.

"Who the hell are you and what the hell are you doing in my office? I will have security escort you out."

"I wish I could say it is a pleasure but that would be a lie. You probably don't recognize me like this." I peeled off the facial prosthetics. "Is this any better or do you prefer the skull face?"

"Young Phillip Baxter, I should've guessed."

"It must be a chilling case of déjà vu for you. This time, a Phillip Baxter is on the other side of the desk. Why are you still standing? Get comfortable, there is much to discuss."

Victor sat desk width apart from me, arms folded and relaxed. I could've easily killed him in 40 different ways and yet he showed no fear. He wasn't remorseful for ruining my chances at a normal life. Victor wrote my life off as an acceptable loss in the grand scheme of things.

"Tell me, Phillip, how does it feel to have real power? It's intoxicating, isn't it? You're taking full advantage of the things my money has afforded you. Aren't you?"

"I'm not here to play your depraved mind games, okay? I am on a righteous path of redemption for my family. I just need some answers from you to complete my journey."

Victor debated the veracity of my claims. "I'll tell you the truth but you have to prepare yourself for what I am about to reveal," he said. "The Black Hand staged the helicopter accident in Vietnam. Southern Vietnamese actors were hired to fake the North's involvement. We released Grandpa Baxter in 1974 to coincide with the actual POW homecoming. It was the first step in the destruction of his fragile psyche. Phillip, the first one, thought the loss of his job was a random occurrence. He knew in his heart he had done nothing wrong. He blamed "the man" and he was right, there was a man behind the scenes ensuring his downfall."

I hated the man before but by now he had my blood boiling. Victor went on to explain the truth behind my grandfather's death. "Your grandpa was good at what he did but your dad was a machine. When your grandpa outlived his purpose, I had him killed. We infected him with cancer during a mandatory physical. We had a young, athletic physical specimen waiting in the wings. I would have been an idiot to squander my investment. Don't misconstrue my words. I grew fond of your grandfather."

I gritted my teeth as I listened to Victor describe his Machiavellian schemes. Once I got him talking, I couldn't get him to shut up. "Your father was something special. He made me billions of dollars from indirect and direct means. His flare and attention to detail made him the perfect mercenary. His only flaw was his heart and no matter how hard I tried to dull his feelings, he still cared. Your father would've crossed me eventually if I hadn't done so first. In the post 9/11 world, he became as obsolete as a typewriter. The age of the highly trained assassin is over. Drones are the new aces because they don't have a conscience. "

"What about my mother? Did you have her killed too?"

"No, don't be absurd. I've always treated my "Reginas" well. The Black Hand didn't plan her death, I promise. The drunk driver who killed her deserves to rot in jail."

"For what it's worth, I believe you."

"How do you think this will end, my boy? The house always wins. Don't you realize you're in my casino?"

"A house is doomed to collapse when it's built with cards. You're living on a shaky foundation and I am here to knock it down."

"I wasn't quite sure until today but you do have the stones for this line of work. There's a place for you here in my organization. We can negotiate."

"No, thanks."

"Don't be so quick to reject the proposal. You have to wonder, where you would be if I hadn't plucked those mulignans out of obscurity?"

Victor fanned the flames of my rage. I rose up, lifted my chair and launched it against the window. A spider web crack formed in the center of the glass. Victor fought me as I dragged him to the window. I smashed his head against the crack repeatedly and shattered the glass. Then, I held him there dangerously close to the edge.

"Do you think this is a joke? You stole every chance I had at happiness." This was the first time he showed any fear in the time that I had been around him. "I am not one to kill in cold blood and you know that, don't you? And yet, I understand how my father killed so easily. He was like a force of nature. No one blames the winter for killing the trees because it's a part of life. You cannot call an earthquake or hurricane evil because it has no morality. That's what my father became because of you. I will teach you no one escapes the hand of death, no matter how much money you have. In the end, your plans and tricks resulted in the creation of a menace known as ACE."

I yanked him closer to the edge of the window. Victor faced the end of his mortality. He bartered his life for what I really wanted, the name of the mercenary who killed my father. I agreed to the exchange. "You must've wondered who tried to snipe you at the restaurant. I'm sure you're aware of Alexander Petrov. The Black Hand secured his release before the execution in Angola. To be clear, Alexander doesn't work for us anymore; he's gone independent and has formed his own mercenary group, the Red Sons. He killed your father and he's going to kill you too. He's a mad man with a score to settle. Alexander will not quit until he wipes out your bloodline." Victor exhaled. "That's everything, okay. Now let me go already."

"I am putting an end to your reign of terror."

"No! No! No! You said you wouldn't--" I removed an ace card from my pocket, inserted it into his jacket and then pushed him out of the window. Victor grasped for anything to latch onto as his body dropped several stories, colliding with the sidewalk. His neck snapped, blood poured into the city's drain system.

"I lied."

"Did you actually push the old man out of the window of his own casino?" Cole said through the earpiece.

"Yeah," I replied.

"Cool."

"Everything's in place, you can send the email now."

"I just emailed the file to my favorite leaking site and every major news organization. It's safe to say it's over, you won."

"I don't feel like a winner."

Voice analysis experts confirmed the authenticity of the file. They used digital software to reduce the background noise and improved the intelligibility of the audio. The audio file implicated 3 former government officials in the conspiracy to assassinate President John F. Kennedy. On the recording, the men admitted to hiring gunmen and tampering with the body.

The revelation reverberated throughout the political landscape. The conspiracy theorists had a field day on social media. One the greatest mysteries of our time had finally been solved.

By now you may have realized you're reading my journal. Each ACE has owned a journal and this one is mine. The therapeutic benefits have done me wonders so far. I'm adding this to the collection for the next ACE.

Guess you're wondering what changed? I didn't go

into the suite planning to kill Victor. When my mother died, I'd thought of death as a menace. Dad's sacrifice taught me that death is the furthest thing from a menace. Death is a gift that reminds us to value each and every day. Without it, we wouldn't view each one as potentially our last. There are real menaces out there like terrorism, racism, sexism, and corruption. These are some of the real menaces, which plague our lives. Hate will never die as long as people accept it as a legitimate part of the human condition. I won't stand by and allow atrocities to continue. I will not have a My Lai on my conscience.

People do not mutilate others without feeling guilt. That's why governments pump billions into propagandizing its citizens against other groups. If you dehumanize another group, it's much easier to sleep at night or to worship at your holy place.

The first two ACEs fought every battle with weapons. I'm different in that regard. I will fight injustice wherever it exists through other means. Yes, I will fight physically but I will also fight through the spreading of knowledge. I am a history teacher and I've pointed out the cyclical nature of history. How many cultures borrowed and improved on the innovations of others. How many wars can you describe by just changing the leader's names and the names of the countries.

This is my penance, the burden that accompanies the Baxter Legacy. I will be a menace to anyone who uses greed to justify his or her evil actions. I may not be able to stop terrorism or racism by myself but I can rid the world of lots and lots of terrorists and racists. Every evil person I remove from this earth helps. I am a force to be reckoned with, reaping what evil has sewn.

CHAPTER 27

FINAL ENTRY

Dear Son,

If you're reading this letter I must be dead. I'm sorry I wasn't able to be part of your life. Words can't express the pain I've felt each and every day since I've parted from your mother's side. There were evil people who stopped me from being there, who ensured I lived a life of unhappiness. The Black Hand Syndicate has eyes and ears at every level of society. Doing what's best for you meant not being your father.

You weren't aware of it but I attended your high school graduation. I sat at the far end of the auditorium, unseen with my baseball cap and video camera. I watched as the other fathers celebrated the occasion with their sons. I had no right to take pride in your accomplishments. That credit belonged to your mother who raised you. I'd like to think that one day you'd find it in your heart to forgive me, though my shame will never allow me to forgive myself.

I hope you don't blame Denise for her part in the deception. She was only doing what was asked of her. Denise's feelings are genuine, which is why I granted her permission to continue the relationship. Treat her well; she's suffered so much in such a short life.

I know the excuses have grown tired. I hate to imagine what you think of me now that the truth has come to light. I've committed unforgivable crimes and for that I will pay, in the next life. Everything I did, all the lives I've taken, were in the name of love.

Your mother did her best to instill you with morals while I amassed a fortune built on blood. Together we provided you with the character and resources to become a hero. The next chapter in the saga of ACE is dependent on you.

Love, Phillip Baxter II

EPILOGUE

I got to know the real Marise, not the Madam Karma persona. She is a good person deep, deep, deep down inside whom hasn't dealt with her childhood trauma. In the end, she managed to get her father's undivided attention. The way I see it, Marise sabotaged her own plans. She assisted my team in dismantling the Black Hand's operations. One day, she'll find the love and acceptance, which has always eluded her.

Madam Karma turned herself in to the Tokyo Police. She admitted to carrying out the political bombings and stealing classified documents. Madam Karma willingly gave up the evidence to the authorities. Her confession exonerated me of the crimes and my espionage charges were dropped. Madam Karma escaped the CIA's custody in route to her maximum-security prison. She is presumably still at large.

Kenzan is actively looking for his eldest daughter. He's convinced he can rehabilitate Marise. I don't think it's my place to dissuade that belief. Kenzan stepped down from his positions at the company and the dojo until further notice.

Denise has made a full recovery, ahead of the doctor's schedule. She's been appointed to the position of Head Instructor at the Kaito dojo. Her lifelong goal has finally been realized. On the off hours, Denise continues to be my partner and friend. Technically, we're more than friends. We've gotten back together. I'm going to fulfill Dad's promise of helping locate her older brother.

Cole's short and long-term memory has improved

dramatically much to the surprise of every so-called expert. The meditation sessions with Kenzan cannot be discounted. He is slowly beginning to trust his own thoughts and memories again. I hired him to be a consultant for the Baxter Production Company. He's added the missing ingredient to the struggling writing team. The CIA experience lent itself greatly to the creative forum. Similarly, to how my father used his experience to produce excitingly authentic movies.

My team has circled the globe to recruiting former spies, soldiers and tech geniuses to aid in my Counter-Assassin crusade. We've formed an international network of lost souls who are no different from ourselves. Former soldiers need a mission and we've given these people something new to fight for.

My definition of Counter-Assassin has broadened to include bettering a life. It used to mean someone who steps in and saves a life or tampers with an assassination attempt. We can rescue people who are essentially dead, living unsatisfying lives. ACE has the means to return happiness, vitality and dignity to these people's lives.

My current and most personal target is Alexander Petrov. He will pay for killing my father and for almost killing me. Alexander has an irrational hate for the Baxter family, which can only end in two ways. He has something coming for him in the form of a bullet. Alexander leads a mercenary team and I have my own. When the planets align I will rip out his heart barehanded.

ABOUT STEVE SAMEDI

Steve Samedi is a licensed mental health counselor who grew up on the Jersey Shore. In the late 70s, his Haitian-born parents came to the United States for better opportunities.

Steve attended Montclair State University where he earned his undergraduate degree in psychology. He went on to study mental health counseling and forensic psychology at the College of Saint Elizabeth. For close to a decade, Steve has worked with various populations ranging from the developmentally disabled to those battling substance addictions.

Steve was inspired to write his first novel during the events of Hurricane Sandy in 2012. He spent a week without electricity and the modern distractions that often hindered the creative process. Steve acted on his childhood dream of creating an iconic character. He crafted a story he believed no one else would have produced. His goal was to breathe life into diverse protagonists that are often underrepresented in popular fiction.

Steve plans to follow-up Menace: The Death Dealer with at least two sequels and a graphic novel.

ABOUT GLOVER LANE PRESS

Thank you so much for your purchase of this amazing debut novel written by Steve Samedi!

Glover Lane Press is thrilled to be the publishing house for this ground-breaking extraordinary work of literary art!

If you enjoyed reading MENACE; The Death Dealer by Steve Samedi, please visit our website for our new, featured and upcoming publications.

Glover Lane Press has helped countless individuals to publish & distribute media independently in print, audio and digital formats.

Visit us at Gloverlanepress.webs.com

Like Us on Facebook:
Facebook.com/Gloverlanepress